Awakening Alice

~~*

A
Ticket
For
Patience

Awakening Alice

~*~

A
Ticket
for
Patience

By

Heather E. Hutsell

Awakening Alice
copyright 2008
2nd Edition
First published 2007
Featured in "Ghost on the Highway"

A Ticket for Patience
1st Edition
First published 2008

All Illustrations by Heather E. Hutsell

ISBN 978-0-6152-1684-3

The two adventures in the pages following are forever dedicated to those whom I have been fortunate enough to laugh, create and cry with. Without you, so many of these crazy moments might never have happened...

~Heather E. Hutsell

Table of Contents

Awakening Alice

A Ticket for Patience

1. Stirring
2. Discovery, The Deaf and Direction
3. Steeping
4. Executioner's Trophy
5. Mixtures and Textures
6. Toads and Cockney Saints
7. Door Hindus and Dog Lemons
8. Missing Beats and Timely Boats
9. Day Dawning and Daunting Dismissed
10. Pins and Needles
11. Kings and Bakers
12. Crooks and Nannies
13. The Dance of the Manti
14. Ockham's Dry-Cutting Razor
15. Tabernacle Yock
16. F.I.R.K.I.N.
    (Found in Restaurant, Killer is Nabbed)
17. Wally Gagging
18. Sweet Treats for Sweet Dreams

Awakening Alice

1. Curiously Reoccurring Arrival

Alice held the limp, stuffed white rabbit under its floppy arms, the never-having-lived body pressed to hers. Again at that place—similar, but not. Different, but not. Things there had once been only pleasantly bright and confusing, colorful and odd. It had changed to something less—a little darker perhaps, but even the Cheshire cat—once a thick-furred tabby (with or without its head) had become rail-thin and ragged. He showed signs of battlement—teeth sharpened, some now missing, and tell-tale tattooing covered the skin on his sparsely furred body.

Whoever had caught the thing? Did it perhaps do all of that scarring to itself?

"Wiser for the wear" the Cheshire had said when Alice had discovered and needlessly freed the beast from a copper samovar that second time around. Or was it *Worn for the wisdom? Word to the wonderer?*

Alice could not remember. It didn't matter. And now here on this third visit—she wondered if she was ever going to see anyone she knew (*knew of*) there? She cast a worried, unamused glance to the ever-changing sky. It fluctuated back and forth between aqua and orange, now and then releasing keys from the heavens. She quickly caught on to take cover under lofty tree branches at those moments--the falling skeleton keys smarted when tinking down on her head.

But it was getting darker now and the ground was softening and getting more difficult to walk on. A few more steps took her onto a large flat rock and she realized that the ground had become a moving river. Her balance teetered and she landed on her backside, the rabbit still in hand. Alice sat still as her raft was carried downstream for a time, the banks' edges too far on either side of her to pull herself to shore just yet.

"There has got to be somewhere that I am headed," she thought to herself. "Because as long as you are *somewhere*, there is always *somewhere else* to go. And I am *somewhere*, but *where*? Certainly not where I was a moment ago!"

And certain objects of oddity began to drift by her then, all in clear, ornate glass bottles with twined tags labeling them. Alice reached less than carefully to pluck one up, the freshly used content steaming up the crystal clearness, so the long, thin object was only a grayish, pinkish blurry thing—

Silver Marrow Knife

And she quickly dropped it back into the water. She had never been terribly fond of anything that had marrow in it. A little extra flavor could just as easily be had with a pinch of salt or a dash of pepper. She supposed it was why grown-ups sometimes found her so incorrigible, the pepper. But the thought of scooping one's marrow caused her very limbs to ache.

She continued to float along, a sudden and distinct change in the objects in the water happening now. The bottles were turning into hand mirrors, all floating as though flat on their backs, and a large green frog hopped from one reflective surface to another as though they were lily pads. It paused as it and Alice crossed one another, its bulgy eyes locking with hers for a moment.

"Don't look too deeply into them—" it croaked. Alice assumed it meant the mirrors, and she leaned over the edge of the rock to the now still water to see her reflection in the glass.

A pale face with blue, red-rimmed eyes stared back at her. She blinked and her eyes traveled down to her neck—it was lined with perfect thick black-stitched 'X's, the line of severage faint but perfectly encircling her throat. She remembered clearly how it had happened:

It had been sunny and warm and she had been watching the fat, fuzzy bumble bees floating around and dipping into the Queen of Hearts' red roses, their legs heavy with saffron-yellow pollen. She had only just reached out to touch one—to see if it really was as furry as it looked, and its intended red-painted-on-white landing pad shattered under her closeness. Alice had heard the Queen wailing before she'd even left the palace, and clouds had rolled in to the command of "*Off with her head!*" Before she knew it, Alice had been bent over a giant deck of cards and with an axe shaped like a spade, her head had been neatly removed with the slightest crunching sounding in her ears. It hadn't hurt, really, but had been deafeningly loud, and the spray had gotten all over her pinafore. How, later it had been reattached—she could not remember.

"Don't look too deeply, I said," the frog was croaking again, as it had hopped back to her. She looked up, startled at the frog's return.

"Well, I suppose I really wasn't looking, since I had got to thinking—"

"Thinking too deeply is as bad as looking too deeply."

The abruptness of it rudely cutting Alice off left her tongue-tied for a moment.

"There is no diff--?"

"No. None."

"Oh—" She was wondering just then if the frog's quick answers were intentional, or was it just plain rude?

"Nope—" it was going on. "—Can't be looking too deeply around here—mark my words—"

"But—"

"Have you got them marked?"

"Well, no. You see, I haven't my pen—"

"Mark them! With dust upon the air if you must!"

Alice looked up into the invisible air in front of her. Her mouth opened to make a remark, but the frog croaked again.

"No! Do not!"

"Well what then, should I be looking at or thinking about?"

"Well anything, really."

Alice sighed and stood up, now that the rock was close enough for her to jump to the embankment. The frog followed, but she tried in earnest to ignore it.

"Where do you go now?" asked the frog.

"I really don't know," admitted an annoyed Alice.

"Well don't you think you should?" it asked, almost before she had finished answering. She stopped, her arms akimbo.
"You really have no sort of manners, interrupting like that, have you?"

The frog blinked at her for a moment before it began to cry.

"Why are you treating me like this?" it sobbed. "I didn't do anything to deserve it!"

And while Alice disagreed, and certainly it had gotten her temper to flare (most definitely the fault of pepper!) she could not help feeling badly at snapping out at it.

"I am sorry, truly," she said. It only sniffed as best as a frog could, and continued to look pathetic. "Please don't be sore at me," she said continuing on.

In the moments of silence that followed, she recalled a conversation from one afternoon while having tea with some of the "grown-ups". There had been a parlor full of ladies, all of them haughtily putting on airs. One was saying to another:

"So she said to Mabel '*I really wish you would stop wearing that frog*--"

And Alice had seen that the woman who had spoken wore a painted broken china frog brooch on her blouse. There was some controversy over the pin and how the woman who had wanted it removed supposedly had "froggy legs" her own self, but she was not insulted by the brooch--rather, she collected frogs and wished for it to be removed and forgotten so she might add it to her menagerie.

"Why don't you talk to me anymore?" the frog suddenly wailed out at Alice. But she supposed answering would only warrant a greater argument about absolutely nothing, and so she went on. She really hoped to eventually run into someone—or thing—that would be worth her talking to. And after all—it was perfectly acceptable to talk to things there! Her first visit had been quite a lot of nonsense, but at least the conversations had been interesting. And now, this time around—and she

15

had only been there a short time as it was, she felt—it had been quite frustrating and pointless. Her head began to hurt some.

"Shall I eat it for you?"

Alice looked back to see the Cheshire cat laying on his back playfully, while dangling the frog by one leg over his wide-opened mouth.

"I don't care."

And perhaps she truly didn't anymore. The cat sat up and studied her for a moment, before giving a shrug and shoving it into his mouth. It made a terrible sound as it went down, but was quickly silenced. For a moment, Alice's stomach turned, but she followed on down the embankment. She supposed she should feel badly that the frog had just been devoured, even if it had been most irritating.

"You're going the wrong way, I think," the cat quipped.

"How do you know?" she asked, perhaps a bit too harshly.

"Now, now--No need to be nasty with *me* about it. I just happen to know that if you keep going *there*, you will run into *Her*, and you don't want to be doing that just yet."

"Well where am I supposed to be going then?" she asked, this time trying to sound a little nicer.

"Over there." And the raggedy cat thumbed over his left shoulder. This brought Alice to stop.

"Why there?"

"Just a suggestion."

But there was a spark in the Cheshire's eyes that got Alice curious.

"And what will I find over that way?"

"Shall we go see?" And already, he was turning in that direction. But to go on, they had to cross the now-solid river, the cat watching that he did not step on the mirrors.

"And mind that you do the same," he said to her. "I am sure you know all about the perils brought on by broken mirrors."

And she did as she was told, crossing the minefield of reflections at long, careful last.

2. Diamond Chips

Alice continued on despite the darkening sky. There seemed to be some sort of glowing coming from deeper within the forest, and knowing that it could be just about anything at that point, she advanced toward it.

There was a wispy sound that grew as she became closer to the luminescence, though there was not even a breeze just then. But only moments later she came upon the source of the glow—a billowing, iridescent, fluffy tentacled tree—a jellyfish tree, to be exact. She stepped around it carefully, not certain if this one would sting her, for she'd heard that jellyfish were capable and tended to do such things when disturbed. It made not a sound, only floated around its trunk--also frosty with opalescence, the branches reaching only slightly toward her but never quite close enough.

"Certainly, it has to sting—" said a voice from nearby. And Alice noticed a queen sitting on a small dune of sand, and digging through the sparkling grains. Alice approached her and saw that she was indeed the Queen of Diamonds.

"Why must it sting?" Alice asked.

"Because it is such a beautiful thing."

The queen continued to run her fingers through the sand, never looking up at Alice.

"And now and then, pretties must sting," she was saying.

"And there is no such thing as gold digging, you know."

Alice noticed then that the queen had several unmatched, broken pieces of china lined up on a piece of fuchsia colored silk, which was spread on her lap. She seemed to be arranging them somehow.

"Oh?" Alice asked.

"There is only piece digging, pieces that don't glow.
Gold diggers get nothing, in the end.
You have to find your own pieces with which to mend."

"Like a puzzle—" Alice said almost excitedly. The queen paused, looking at Alice then for a moment, a long flame red curl falling from beneath her bejeweled crown. Her eyes quickly went back to her task at hand.

"If that is what you truly wish:
glue them together and make a dish."

"Well, they are from dishes it would seem," Alice said matter-of-factly, not sure if she liked that the queen spoke—nearly sang in rhyme. But it was catchy. Alice dug her toe into a little mound of sand, pushing out a chip of white china with part of a green leaf on it.

The queen noticed it and reached out, her hand stopping before she could rudely take it. Alice pulled her foot back quickly.

"Oh! You may have it." And the queen took it for her collection.

"Have you been at this long?" Alice asked.

Time, I do not recollect.
But hours I spend in circumspect.
Boxes at home I completely fill.
And many moments with this task I kill."

Alice looked on for a moment in silence, not seeing much hope for the Queen of Diamonds making much of a sensible picture with what she had.

"I'm afraid your findings are in vain—" she began, but stopped. She knew she ought to know better by now and hold her tongue, especially when it came to speaking with the adults. And from high up in another tree, the Cheshire cat looked down on them, clucking his tongue at her and shaking his head.

"My search may be in vain, tis true,
But closer I am to riches than you."

Perhaps, Alice thought, she was a queen after all. But she didn't think the woman needed to sound smug about it. She felt like voicing that opinion as well, but saw the Cheshire cat take a leap into the top of the jellyfish tree, the ends fluffing up suddenly like a pile of feathers, and she wanted to see if he came out of it all right. He did not appear immediately but she could see the bottoms of his feet indenting the top of the jellies from the underside.

"How do you manage to rhyme all day long?" Alice asked. "Or do you?"

"By rhyming I keep my thoughts my own,
and shall continue till my lips are sewn.
With not a soul daring to end
what they themselves cannot pretend:
That the precious magic to our being,
is the music that your heart is seeing."

The Queen of Diamonds looked up at Alice again then.

"You'll understand what I say, little one,
I hope before your days are done,
If you haven't listened to your heart,
like these cups, you'll come apart.
But now is not the time to fret—"

And she rose to her feet and dusted off her long beautiful fingers. Alice wondered if the woman liked to play the piano. And as she continued speaking, she placed a china chip in Alice's hand with those long fingers.

"Or ponder on the weight future regret,
but see some things that make you wary,
and are far from ordinary.
Look through there in trees beyond,
past the needles around the pond,
And meet with someone very wise:
A brassy lizard with ruby eyes.
He's got a story to fancy your ears
And maybe bring your laughter to tears.

19

Be certain to have him play his cello,
The one of silk that is painted yellow.
It's full of water and sounds as such,
But the song he'll play you'll love so much."

At this point the Queen of Diamonds began to smile. Alice could tell that this lizard the queen spoke of must be rather talented, or at least some kind of close friend to her. She got such a look in her eyes when speaking of him. Alice left her then, turning back once to see that the queen still stood, waving at Alice, and once again moments later to see that she had gone back to her treasure hunting. The queen had been most beautiful, yet a strange and hopeful sadness shone behind the sea green of her eyes. Alice had never seen the sea, but imagined it to be the same color as the queen's eyes. It made her wonder what the King of Diamonds was like.

3. Tales for Tails

Alice paused to check her whereabouts then. All along one side of the path was a row of sharp, brightly glinting embroidery needles, all of them easily four feet tall where they stuck out of the ground. And the pond the Queen of Diamonds had mentioned lay just behind it. She wondered if she had gotten smaller yet again, but everything else seemed to be of normal size. It was only the needles that seemed out of place. To her right were diamond-shaped patches of lobelias and it looked to Alice that this part of the place was given great care. Her mother had always included lobelias in her garden, Alice recalled. But they never seemed to look quite so thriving as these.

"They must be very well loved," she said out loud.

"And so they are!" said a very Scottish sounding voice from behind the needle hedge.

"Who said that?" asked Alice.

"Why I did, of course."

Alice looked in the direction of the voice but saw only a waving walking stick behind the needles. She followed along them, looking for a way to get on the other side. But they went on for quite a while.

"Well, come so I can see you—"

"Patience, patience, miss. The name's Toby, by the by. And you must be Miss Alice-?"

Alice wanted more than ever to see whom she was talking to!

"How did you know my name? Have we met?"

"No, my dear. But I have already heard all about you. Here, now lass—" and the walking stick waved to her several feet down the row. "Almost there now."

"Whom do we know in common?"

"Why, my dear queen! Of Diamonds, that is."

"Oh! The lizard!" she said, knowing he must be the storyteller the queen had mentioned.

"For certain, my dear. Ah!"

And from around the end of the needles, stepped a finely dressed lizard, his scales shining golden in the sun and his eyes flashing just like a pair of perfect rubies. He pointed his hippopotamus-handled walking stick at her and grinned.

"Just as beautiful as she'd said as well, ah!" he scurried to her and shook her hand excitedly. "Come along now, come along!"

21

They sat on giant pincushions. Alice thought them to look like huge tomatoes only covered in red felt. Thankfully, there were no pins in them.

"So, how have you been?" Toby asked her with great interest. "How are your lessons?"

"Well, I suppose. Though I have been here instead of there, and don't much remember when my last lesson was. Nor what it was about for that matter."

"Ah, I see. Well, no mind then."

"The queen said I am to have you tell me a story."

"Oh did she now? Hm. Well, were you thinking of a long tail?" and he held up his own tail and this brought a smile to Alice's lips. "Or must it be a short one?" At this, he held the handle end of his walking stick to Alice and turned it around. Not only did the knob have a hippopotamus's head, but a quick spin showed that it also had a backside. And at the word *tale*, it began to wag its own tail.

"Oh, well, I'm not sure."

"Well, how much time have you got?"

"I don't know that either, sir. I am sorry."

"Oh, no bother, no bother. Hm. Best to make it a short one then. But for that, I shall need Clemens to wake up. He must help to tell it, as you see—the short tail belongs to him."

What Alice knew just then, was that there were a lot of *tales* and *tails* involved with her having sat down with this lizard! She hoped he didn't ask to see *her* tail. She wasn't sure how she would approach such a request.

"Clemens! Clem, darling. Wake up!"

The hippopotamus's eyes did open then and very wide at that when he saw Alice.

"*I don't believe it!*" he exclaimed.

"Clem, dear, this is *Our* Alice, and we're going to tell her a story."

"Oh! Oh! A story! For the girl! *I don't believe it!* This is going to be *wonderful!*"

"Yes, yes. Of course it will be!" and Toby smiled at Alice. "We need a short one now."

"Oh, yes! Yes, a short one! Oh! Get your cello! It will be wonderful!"

"I shall get it, love. But will you behave yourself do I put you down?"

"Yes, yes! Oh I will be *ever* so good! I can't *believe* it!"

Alice could not help smiling at the strange pair, and she realized as Toby propped the stick against his giant tomato to reach for his cello, that her cheeks were beginning to hurt already. From somewhere behind the tomato, a canary yellow cello was born and Toby held it gingerly, the strings being made of some type of kelp, dripping with beads of water. And for the bow, his long tail, of course.

"Let me tune up now—" he was saying, and Clemens's tail was wagging wildly. Alice thought the hippo would jump off of the walking stick and run around if he could. Toby took a strum and the cello let out a fine, even wail, not at all offensive to Alice's ears. He grinned at her and gave the seaweed strings a pluck.

"*Weelll*—!" Toby started quite suddenly, making Alice jump. Of course, this made her laugh too.

"*There once was a Man who lived in the Moon*—

And jolly was his demeanor
When tipping back snifters of choc'lat as was his boon
No one could say t'was of cheese
His home—no, no one could say it was made of cheese—"

And here Clemens joined in:

"No one could say it was made of cheese—of cheese
No, ne'er was it made of cheese!"
Clemens quieted for the second verse.
"Well, one day a nanny goat came alongside the moon
Her 'tensions were naught but of evil
She prom'sed to knock it from the sky and soon—
But instead took an invite from Be-el—zabub
Beelzebub, Beelzebub, and quickly did she go—"

And Clemens joined in again:

"Right down to a fiery, blasted pit
She didn't even have a basket—"

Clemens solo: *"a basket, a basket!"*
And together: *"slipped right down to the blazing inferno*
Faster than were she to slide—"

Toby paused and Clemens continued:

"Right out of an eel's bottom!"

Alice could not help but to burst out laughing, but the duo
would not quit.

"With the evil nanny out of the way
The Man in the Moon did thrive
Along came a pretty sweet pea one day,
And he kept her at his side—
His side, his side!
She was his beautiful bride!
Forever and ever and ever his bride
Let's have some wine and cheese!"

And Alice laughed until her sides ached, because while it made no sense at all, it still made perfect sense and she quite nearly fell off of her pincushion at the wonderful story.

"Well now, what did you think of that?" Toby asked her.

"It was *wonderful!*" Clemens shouted, wiggling on the walking stick. "*I can't believe it! Wonderful!*"

Alice still laughed, holding her sides.

"Did you like it?" Toby asked, patting Clemens's head.

"Oh, but it *was* wonderful!" She agreed, wiping tears from her eyes. "It was lovely! I should so like to meet the Man in the Moon some day."

Toby leaned close to speak softly near her ear.

"And perhaps some day, my dear, you shall!"

"I think his sweet pea must be ever so—yes, ever so lovely!" Clemens sighed, tilting his head pensively.

"Why of course she is," Toby insisted. "Do you have time for another story, lass?"

"Oh," Alice said sadly, "I am afraid that I probably don't." Though this was true, she could hardly think of a reason why.

"Well, another time then."

It was then that the sky began to darken and lighten alternately, with something akin to lightening flashing overhead, and Alice looked up at it, half expecting to see the clouds billowing hither and thither. What she saw was a bit more shocking and she nearly dropped to her knees at the sight, her arms over her head in an attempt to protect it. Certainly she would have gone completely to the ground, had Toby had not steadied her.

"Do not worry, lass. It's *animal crackers.*"

But what Alice saw hardly looked like animal crackers—or any kind of crackers, for that very matter! What they looked like—the giant, white gracefully swarming creatures—were some kind of crisp, fluid dragons. They figure-eighted around one another endlessly, the three of them. They would, now and again make a plunging dive, but always they would dive back up to a safer height, not coming anywhere close to the ground.

"*Animal cr-crackers?*" Alice said.

"Just an expression, my dear!" Toby said. "They are completely and utterly harmless!"

"Are you sure?" Alice asked softly. "But they are dragons."

"Why they are simply *Origami dragons.*"

"Where do such things come from, I wonder?"

"Who knows?" he said, not appearing to be the slightest bit concerned about them or the fact that they kept blocking out the daylight. "But they are made of rice paper. They will melt when it rains."

And who knew when that would be? Alice thought, as there was not a single or even the slightest hint of a cloud in the sky just then.

"Will I be safe to go on?" she asked. "Do you think?"

"Of course, lass. Do come back again when you can stay for a longer time!" Toby invited.

She promised to do just that but began on her way after thanking Toby and Clemens again for their story, the *animal crackers* expression still crunching in her mind. She wondered if *animal crackers* was the same as *piece of cake*? In a manner of speaking, of course. But then, animal crackers weren't really crackers, so much as they were cookies, and cookies were generally sweet like cake, so she guessed that perhaps it did mean the same thing.

As she went along her way, she thought about the dragons and what would happen to them once it rained. How sad! Such beautiful creatures melting at the wet assault, even if they were rather intimidating. But the farther she got from Toby and Clemens and the lobelia garden, the less likely it looked to rain. In fact—it looked as though rain was the farthest thing from happening, ever again.

4. Join the Club

Alice noticed that the sun was quickly reaching its timely and very hot, hot peak, causing a little trickle of perspiration to run down off of the tip of her nose. It certainly was the warmest day she'd ever spent in that place. At least that she could, in her short memory recall.

A nice day for a swim, she was thinking to herself. *And not at all a good one for petticoats and the absurdity of the like!*

For this thought, it was no wonder that her little brows rose as she came upon another queen—this one dressed in closely fitted, heavy black and white checkered velvet. The queen had her back to Alice, but appeared to be speaking—to herself, Alice presumed—and quite heatedly besides. Alice did not know whether she ought to approach her further, for though the Queen of Diamonds had seemed pleasant, her experience with the Queen of Hearts had been quite different. On the other hand, she supposed no one particularly like being sneaked up upon either. So she circled half the way to the queen's right side and waited as patiently as she could to be addressed.

The argument, Alice noted, was with a looking glass, which the queen held in her hand. Or at least it was with whomever appeared to the queen in its reflection. Alice also saw that the queen's mirror as well as two others, were attached with satin ribbons of aqua blue, melon orange and lemon yellow by their handles, and those connected to a firmly sewn ring at the queen's waist.

"But *darling*," she was saying. "You won't even know that I'm there. *Really*—" –insisted. "You won't notice me *at all.*"

She then lowered the mirror slowly as she felt Alice's eyes on her. The queen spun around with all quickness, the checkered skirt splitting down the middle to reveal a large black club on a blindingly white satin underskirt. Dark and obsidian-sharp eyes fell on Alice and she had to step back, for fear of them slicing into her.

"*Well,*" the queen said saucily. "Who might you be?" Alice could tell by the queen's voice that she could have answered with the *Mother of all Creation*, and it would not have impressed the woman in the least.

"Alice." And she was right.

"Hm." Not interested what ever so. The queen lowered the looking glass on the yellow ribbon and raised one from the orange ties. There was a club and a dagger embossed on the back, and she flipped it over abruptly.

"With whom were you speaking?" Alice began. "If you don't mind my asking, of course—"

The queen seemed not to have heard her, for she continued to look into the glass. But after a moment, she did look at Alice and glared at her before smiling widely.

"Of course I mind your asking! Wouldn't you?"

"Well—" *No*, Alice thought to herself. She would not have minded at all!

"Why, my husband, *darling!*" the queen said then.

"Husband? Is it a magic mirror?"

"I suppose. I want to go on a hunting expedition with him, but—" she sighed with a pout and quite dramatically besides. "He says I cannot."

"Hunting for what?"

"Hm. Kind of nosey, aren't you?" Alice felt the sting behind the question, but did not dare to budge from it. "For dead men."

Alice knew better than to think she had heard incorrectly. But the question now—who was dead? The hunting or the hunted? But the queen would not leave any room for question in the girl's mind. Again, she looked into the glass, this time, pinching her pale cheeks to make them red.

"My husband is dead. They all are. Well, except the one." She held a limp lime green ribbon and Alice could see that there was no mirror at its ends.

"How many do you have?"

"Three so far." And the mirror lowered once more. "How many do *you* have?"

By the tone of her voice, Alice felt she should have many as well, and yet Alice wondered why the queen would ask her that—could she not see that she was very young? But she supposed that kings and queens did marry very young, though this queen looked rather worn for her age.

"Well," she began. "I suppose, I have none."

"Oh." And up went the mirror. "I imagine you and *Spades* will have much in common then."

Alice figured she could only mean the Queen of Spades by this, but she said nothing.

"I'm *going* on that expedition—trust me. And I have my own court, you know. He'll have nothing to say about it because what is it that they say?"

"I don't know, your majesty."

"Exactly, you wouldn't," she snapped. But then—"You poor dear girl. I am positively sure you couldn't possibly be content, as you are—not married, I mean. I do know a few Jacks that I could introduce you to."

She sighed quite impatiently then and lowered the orange, exchanging it for the aqua.

"Oh," Alice said. "But I'm not really interested, I don't thin—"

"Yes you are, trust me." And the queen turned her back on Alice.

"Well, I won't be staying, you see—"

"You *will*. And you'll love him and he'll love you, you'll see!" The queen faced her again, shaking the mirror at Alice as though it were an extension of her finger. She reminded Alice of her schoolmaster just then by doing so. "You have to be persistent and not give up. It's quite worth the humiliation of being refused over and over again—*trust me*."

Alice did not like it much when the schoolmaster called upon her in class to answer questions in the lesson and she suffered the humiliation of answering incorrectly. Certainly she would like it much less so—the humiliation in regard to something so delicate. It was time to be leaving, she decided, before things got any more uncomfortable.

"Well, your majesty—" and the queen seemed to stand taller, to puff out more widely, more proudly at the address. "I should be going now. It was nice to meet you—" and she turned quickly to leave.

"*Stop!*" Alice froze, feeling the queen rushing up behind her. "You will not leave yet."

"Oh, but I must! I-I—"

"You *nothing*. Take this—" it was an order. "A gift," the queen was saying, her voice suddenly sugary sweet. She raised a red ribbon from her girdle and snipped off a few inches with her fingernails, which suddenly looked to Alice like a pair of sewing pincers. The motion was so fast, Alice could not be certain. She took the ribbon and quickly dropped it into her empty pocket, the soft fibers feeling like razors, and then she pulled her hand out and held it behind her back, out of the queen's view. She was growing quite uncomfortable under the queen's increasing and overbearing smugness, and the woman was beginning to look as though she was swelling all over. Alice feared the woman would eventually explode, did she stay there much longer!

"Thank you, your majesty. Good day!"

And she turned and ran as fast as she could, slowing only once she was certain that she was far enough away and out of the queen's sight. She then held her hand in front of her, fingers still clenched and little streams of blood dripping from between them. Certainly the ribbon could not have done that, could it have? But paper, she had learned, could leave a most nasty cut if it got you just right. So why not a ribbon?

Curious.

No. This was not curious. This was bad. Very, *very* bad.

Alice wiped her bloodied hand on the underside of her pinafore, the cuts having been quite deep. She would have thrown the ribbon away just then, had she not been afraid to reach for it. And was it truly as sharp as she'd imagined, she supposed it might eventually cut its way out of her pocket.

What had it been about the Queen of Clubs that had made her hair stand on end anyway? Alice could not put her finger on it. But certainly, not even the Queen of Hearts, with her pension for lopping off heads at a moment's fancy could be considered so oddly and deeply evil.

5. Small Talk

Alice continued on, a little more slowly now, looking up at the sky for a moment and seeing that it was turning pink and stretching farther away from her. Or perhaps she was shrinking again. She stopped to lean against a tree and removed her shoe to shake a few pebbles out of it, one of them plinking down on the head of an ant nearly three feet long, who happened to be passing by at just that very moment.

"Oh bother," she sighed—shortened again, for sure.

"*Ouch!*" yelped the ant.

"Oh! I am *so* terribly sorry, sir!" she said, outstretching her hand toward it, but wondering if it was wise to rub its poor bumped head.

"Not a problem miss," it said. "Just watch where you are flinging those. Ta now! Bye-bye!"

And the ant trundled on along its way. Alice just watched it go, but suddenly ran to catch up with it and they began to walk side by side.

"Ah. Going my way?" the ant remarked.

"Well," Alice began. "I don't really have a way right now. Would you mind the company?" She felt she ought to be as polite as can be after causing it such harm!

"Not at all. Just try to keep up—lots to do."

Alice would try to keep up, but the pebbles had made little blisters on her feet and it was terribly painful to walk. But the ant seemed jollier than some of the others she had encountered, and she decided it would be worth the suffering just the same.

"Where are you headed?" she asked it. "You seem to be in a great hurry."

"I am. Winter is coming, you know."

"Is it?" But of course she knew it was—in several more months. "Are you gathering for your—*hibernation*?"

"I am the scout." And it said *scout* rather proudly. "And we don't really hibernate, *per se*. But the stocking up is quite necessary."

"Oh."

"I happen to know where all the best places are for food and such. I always do," it said, throwing her a glance. "In case you feel like doing a little stocking up for yourself," it added.

Alice figured she could *stock up* about as much as her two dress and two pinafore pockets would hold. Certainly it would not be enough to get her through any winter. Perhaps not even enough for a week! Rather, she hoped she would be getting to a dining table at some point in the nearer that farther future. Already she had missed more tea times than she could count and she thought perhaps she might be getting a bit peckish. She did not care so much for the tea as she missed eating the tiny sandwiches and cakes that went along with it. She supposed the ant would find something like those to nibble on appealing and she was sorry she had none with her. Still, she could find no reason in not bringing them up.

"Do you like canapés?" she asked. The ant's head tilted in question.

"Couldn't say for certain. What is it?"

"Well, they're like sandwiches. Little ones that you could stuff entirely into your mouth all in one bite."

"Oh."

"They sometimes have cucumbers or pate on them—that's French, you know. For *goose*."

"Is that so?"

"They are quite delicious."

"Sounds like it."

"And we have little sweet cakes with them as well. Do you like cake?"

"Very much. But I prefer mine a crumb at a time."

"Frosted or plain? Sometimes they are made with preserves in between the layers and I do very much enjoy—"

"Hush—!" the ant interrupted suddenly. And they both stopped walking. Alice tipped her head to the side, straining to hear what the ant obviously heard quite clearly.

"What is it?" Alice whispered. The ant's antennae twitched for a moment, Alice still hearing nothing.

"Weeping."

"Weeping?"

"Come along," the ant said softly.

It led the way, Alice lingering behind, not sure if she wanted to witness someone's obvious despair. She didn't feel that she was very good at lending much support for that.

"Oh. We're too late," the ant said simply, and this brought Alice rushing to its side.

Between a few towering tiger lilies, lay a man—clearly once a king—with a dagger plunged through his head.

6. A Spade for the Grave

"Well. Finally did himself in, I see," said a newcomer to Alice and the ant.

A woman dressed in all black and with a lace mantilla over her head had joined them. She crouched down next to the dead king and lifted her veil back, exposing her pale, beautiful face. Her lips were blood red and her eyes were like cobalt glass. She stood with a sigh and flung the king's cape over his head. Then turning to Alice and the ant, she beamed with a smile.

"I haven't seen you before," she said to Alice. Remembering her manners then, Alice curtsied.

"I'm Alice, your majesty."

"Well, nice to meet you. I'm sure you can guess who I am."

And truly Alice figured her to be the Queen of Spades, for she was the only queen of the deck that Alice had not yet met.

"Yes, your majesty."

"I am sorry you had to see that." The queen put out her hand for Alice to take and the woman led her away from the dead king.

"Why do you think he did that? If I may ask," she asked.

"For precisely the very reason I have no king of my own." Alice gave her a puzzled look. "It is a little complicated. But I will try to explain, if you have the time."

"Yes, of course."

"If you don't mind," the ant began. "I will be on my way. Plenty to do, you know."

"Certainly," the queen excused him.

"Thank you kindly, your grace," the ant said. "Nice to meet *you*," he said to Alice. "Ta now! Bye-bye!"

The queen sat down on a rock, spreading out her black lacy skirts like a frothy ebony sea around her. Alice thought her to look like an exquisite black rose opening its petals. (She'd never seen a black rose but she was sure that it would be exactly that lovely!) At the queen's inviting hand, she sat on the grass, her legs crossed under her own blue skirt.

"You may have heard the story of the stolen tarts--?" the queen began.

"Yes, I think so," Alice said. "But I couldn't begin to remember how it goes right now. I always seem to have that kind of trouble here."

"Well, I shall tell it all to you. It goes as such:

The Queen of Hearts
She baked some tarts
All on a summer's day.
The knave of Hearts
He stole the tarts
And took them clean away.
"Give me my tarts,
Oh Knave of Hearts,"
The Queen of Hearts said she.
"I'll give you your tarts,
Oh Queen of Hearts
If only you'll come with me."
So the Knave of Hearts
Took the Queen and her tarts
All on a summer's day.

And the King of Hearts
Who had lost his smarts
From the Queen having gone away,
Took his dagger of hearts
Shaped like most darts
And put it into his head.
Now while the Knave of Hearts
And the Queen with her tarts
Live happily,
The King is quite dead."

Alice waited for a moment to see if there was more, but the queen did not say anything.

"How dreadful!" she commented then.

"Perhaps," sighed the queen.

"But the last time I saw the Queen of Hearts, she was not so very happy," Alice noted, thinking of the poem explaining the queen's delight.

"Perhaps, again. Love is so very complex," the queen said, leaning slightly forward.

"Did you once have a king, your majesty?" she asked, thinking of the Queen of Clubs, who seemed to have enough kings for all of that strange world.

"Thankfully not."

"But there *is* a King of Spades, isn't there?"

"Of course, dear. But we are not married. He is my brother."

Alice was most confused at this. She wondered where in the world Kings of Spades would come from then. The queen anticipated this question and answered it without hesitation.

"From rocks."

"Rocks? What kind of rocks?"

"Very special ones, of course."

Well, Alice would be most careful, the next time she decided to walk around kicking rocks over! One would never know if they were kicking around kings, would they? She supposed she might but after the fact, for they would certainly let out some kind of holler—wouldn't they?

"You have not long ago met with the Queen of Clubs, haven't you?" asked the Queen of Spades.

"Why, yes. However did you know?"

"Your dress is soiled."

36

The queen stood and began to look around at their surroundings, and Alice's eyes dropped down to the drying blood on her lap.

"She says that *I* am an *Old Maid*. A *spinster*—" her eyes glanced back at Alice with amusement. "But she is the one that spins, like a black widow. Webs of deceit all around her." She shook her head, looking at some flower seeds that were the size of her palm. "Miserable hag. Do be wary of her, when you encounter her again."

"I hope not to."

"You most likely will. And do not believe her lies. Greater is the deceiver who asks for your trust without earning it first." She motioned for Alice to come to her and the girl bound to her feet obediently. The queen broke the pod open and pulled out long white, cottony fibers, handing three of them to Alice. "She does not like anyone and she will do anything to cause pain, even if it appears as though she is doing something favorable and lovely."

"What are these for?" Alice held up the feathery seedlings.

"A most peculiar purpose, which I cannot explain to you at this time—mostly because you'd not believe me if I told you. But when you need them, you will know."

Alice put them in one of her dress pockets, wondering how she would ever find them again, should she resume her normal size.

"And for goodness sake—remember never to place them too closely to your nose," the queen warned. Alice would be certain that she would do no such thing! Even holding a flower against her nostrils would make her sneeze. Of course, that had much to do with her always picking the ones with a little bit of dew in them, and perhaps that she always inhaled a little too deeply. Only once or twice had she actually sniffed in a bug, but she didn't figure that to happen with these little things.

"Yes, your majesty."

"Good. Now then, take a walk with me."

Alice hesitated.

"Something wrong, my dear?" the queen asked.

"But, what about--?" And she pointed to the dead King of Hearts, who just then looked like a big red velvet lump.

"Oh. Your ant friend will come back for him."

"But won't he be getting a proper burial?"

The queen thought on that for a moment.

"Well, I suppose that he will. Returned to under the rock from whence he came, I imagine. Come along." And she offered her arm to Alice and the girl linked up with her obediently.

"Where are we off to?"

"You shall see."

"Is it a surprise?" Alice asked, uncertain if she wanted any more surprises.

"Of a sort. You must remember, my dear, that life is full of surprises. And I think you shall like this one."

7. Texas Tea

The Queen of Spades led Alice out of the glade and into an open and sparse sandy terrain. There was very little else there with them, and the sun beat down on everything beneath it. Still, it was not overly hot. Alice hoped they would find some kind of shade however, for the brightness was making her eyes water terribly, and the only trees were of a more prickly sort without any branches or leaves. She remembered seeing a picture of something similar to these—cactuses, they were. Upon closer inspection, she saw that there were tiny blue flames coming from each sharp barb. She made a point not to keep her distance, not wanting to get singed and most likely she would if she got too close.

"What are we to find here?" She asked the queen. She wondered should she dread the answer, but truthfully she was feeling quite comfortable with this queen and did not fear that any harm would come to her so long as she remained in her majesty's company.

"You shall see. I'm certain that he's around here somewhere—"

And at that, Alice began to look around for whoever *he* was. The queen waited a moment more, with her hands on her hips and then she gave Alice a smile before cupping her hands next to her mouth to whistle loudly. A few more moments passed before they spotted a dark four-legged creature off in the distance. It ambled toward them, almost trotting, its short legs looking a bit wobbly as it carried its oblong form across the sand. The queen smiled at its arrival, and the closer it got, the more clearly they could see that it carried something of sizable notice on it's bluish back.

"Well, whatever has kept you, Georgie?" the queen asked, though she seemed not in the least upset with the tardy animal.

"How'do, Ma'am. Do pardon my keepin' you a'waitin'."

The odd animal reached them then, and Alice could see that the object on his back was quite actually the Cheshire cat. The feline hopped down, walking gingerly over the warm ground. Georgie seemed not at all to have noticed that the cat had stowed away on him.

Alice realized as he now stood at their feet, that his body was covered in rows of protective navy blue plates, each embossed with poppy-like floral patterns. A long, rat-like tail stuck out from under one end of the shell and his pointed nose led his head out from the other end. Alice had never seen such a thing, but it seemed harmless enough and certainly it was very well mannered.

"Georgie, this is Alice," the queen introduced.

"Ma'am," he greeted. And Alice was positive that if he had a hat, he would have tipped it to her. He seemed less than excited about her being there, but suddenly came to a realization of some sort and stood straight up on his hind legs at fully direct attention. Alice thought this to look quite ridiculous, as it made Georgie's nose point ever exactly skyward. She nearly expected him to stake himself into the ground with his long rigid tail, like a fat sausage on a skewer.

"By *golly*, she's *Her!*" he exclaimed.

The Cheshire cat yawned and leaned against the flaming cactus (not noticing that it scorched some of his remaining fur) and rolled his eyes.

"Is it time for tea yet?" the cat asked, ignoring the situation all together.

Alice leaned close to the queen, and spoke in a low voice, so as not to insult Georgie.

"Your majesty, if you please—what *is* he?"

Georgie dropped down onto all fours once more with a soundful thud and looked at Alice just as inquisitively.

"Georgie is an—"

"An armadille, ma'am."

"An *armadille*?" Alice said.

"Or crocodillo, if you prefer," the Cheshire car offered, sounding quite bored of it all.

"Why that sounds an awful lot like croco*dile*," Alice noted.

"If it is your pleasure, ma'am."

"But—*why* are you called that?"

And to acknowledge Alice's query, Georgie opened his mouth quite wide and quite unexpectedly, showing a multitude of sharp, white teeth. Alice gasped and leapt backward and Georgie clamped his mouth closed as quickly as he'd opened it.

"Why, ma'am, I would never use these to harm you," he promised, his long drawling voice making Alice curl her tongue behind her closed lips to imagine imitating his speech.

"How's about that tea?" the Cheshire interrupted, imitating the drawl.

"Really, cat," the queen began, sitting on the sand. "You are so inappropriately thirsty sometimes."

"And you, extraordinarily lacy, my queen."

Alice wasn't sure if his remark was meant to be an insult, for the queen's gown *was* layers and layers of lace, and she really didn't seem to mind the comment at all.

"Georgie--?" she began instead.

"Why, I'd be only too happy to oblige—"

With his long tail, he reached into the sand and in turn, pulled out four teacups. An image of the Queen of Diamonds flashed through Alice's mind just then, the tea cups in the sand reminding her of the broken china the queen had been searching for. She made to say something about it, but the Cheshire cat began talking to the Queen of Spades instead.

"I heard that ol' Hearts cleaved his brain pan today."

"You heard right," she said, taking the teacup from Georgie. It had steaming tea in it, which most obviously had come from a teapot also drawn from the sand. Alice decided that she must pay closer attention to this! Imagine—hot black tea coming from the ground! Thought she thought it too sound a bit absurd—how could she not believe her own eyes?

"Pitiful," the cat said, taking his now-filled cup from Georgie's tail with his own. She tried with utmost diligence to pay attention to the conversation, as she truly wanted to know what was being said. Though as well, she wanted to watch for where the tea had come from, for one could never be too careful when accepting tea from a near stranger.

"I suppose he's better off," the cat said. "The queen could be so temperamental sometimes. It would have been a only matter of time before she would have done it to him, herself." At this statement, the Cheshire cat winked at Alice and her hand immediately went to her throat. The stitching had fallen off at some point in time, though she had made no notice of it until now. All that remained were the smooth scarred dots of the needle punctures.

"Nice perforation," the Cheshire said to Alice. "Good guide lines for next time."

The queen clicked her tongue and shook her head.

"Not terribly tactful, my dear," she said to him. The cat drained his cup and set it on Georgie's head like a helmet, just as Georgie poured sand from the pot into Alice's cup and then handed it to her. She took it, expecting it to be full of sand, but there was instead steaming tea in it, just as there should be.

"I do hope you like it sweet, ma'am," Georgie said.

"Oh, of course," she said, paying more attention to the Cheshire cat. "Thank you."

41

"My pleasure. It's the hottest tea there is this side of the Sar-ha. It never gets cold."

"I suppose not—" Alice muttered. She turned to the queen and the Cheshire cat.

"So, now that the King of Hearts is--dead," Alice began, her tea certainly too hot to drink just yet. "What will happen to the Queen? Will she rule her kingdom by herself? Will it now become a--*queendom*?"

"Oh no," said the cat. "She can't rule anymore. Well, not like before."

"Oh?" the queen said with interest. "What ever could stop her, I wonder?"

"Well, you see," he began, climbing up onto the queen's lap and laying on his back, all paws up in the air. "She's lost her head."

"Lost *her* head!" Alice cried in sudden surprise.

"Well, it fell off, actually." The cat pawed at the corner of the Queen of Spade's mantilla nonchalantly. "She keeps it in a giant bougainvillea."

And Alice had no idea what a *bougainvillea* might be.

"Why that's a mighty pretty flower, ma'am," Georgie offered, the teacup still on his head. "Kind of paper lantern-like."

"Which reminds me—" The Cheshire sat up, gave a half-snort, half-purr and rubbed his nose against the queen's chin, surprising even her, before jumping down onto the ground.

"*Queenie* told me to give you this—"

He began to cough and hack, the queen rolling her eyes at such a grotesque display, and in moments the Cheshire had brought up a sizable hairball and he deposited at Alice's feet. She merely looked at it, not at all in a hurry to touch the slimy thing.

"Please," the cat said, his voice edged with sarcasm. "*Allow me.*"

He began to pull it apart with his claws, but in those few seconds, it had turned into a smooth, sky blue egg and the shell cracked open easily. Inside, there was a small heart made of what looked like polished red rock.

"It's supposed to open, but don't ask me how. She really didn't explain."

"Whatever is it for, I wonder?" Alice said, though more to herself of course.

"She didn't elaborate on that either." The cat jumped back up onto his mistress's lap. "Just that it'll come in handy with whatever *Red* gave you."

"*Red?*"

42

"Her majesty of Diamonds, of course."

"Oh." Alice paused for a moment. "But why would she—after—?" and she touched her neck lightly.

"Help you?" he finished for her.

"Yes—" her voice had become soft. "Why would she help me?"

The cat shrugged and curled up, yawning again.

"Maybe she had a change of *heart*."

The queen cocked her brow at the word play, but then smiled at Alice, the shine in her blue eyes showing that she definitely agreed.

"Accept the gift, my dear," the queen said. "If she knows anything, then certainly she knows what she's talking about."

Alice picked it up, feeling a faint but constant pulse coming from somewhere inside of it. She wondered—if she'd lost her head—the Queen of Hearts, then did that also mean that was she dead? But the cat had said that *she* kept it in a bougan-whatsit, as though there were some choice to the matter. And the rest of her body—? Where would she keep *it*? And when Alice herself had lost her head—was there a time when her body had roamed around without her head? What kind of things could she have done? There would have been no use in having tea, and she could not have done any reading, for how could she have read *and* turned the pages? Unless of course she had been just beside her own head or holding her own head and just *what* kind of a trick would that have been to perform?

Alice sighed. There was too much to try to understand in that, and had she not learned better of that place by now? That there was no making sense of such things?

"Do share with us, Alice dear, what is in your head," the Queen requested, the conversation having taken a pause and all eyes suddenly on Alice.

"Well, that is just the complication of it—I was thinking about when I had *no* head. Do you suppose I was able to *think at all?* Certainly, I would not have bothered with arrowthematics or theories of relatives or anything of that sort—*would* I have?"

Her loyal audience said nothing for a moment, Alice's baffling rant bouncing about in their own heads just then like a fly in a little wooden pig toy.

"*No*" "*Certainly probably not*" "*Not likely*" all came at once.

"I do so wonder then, what I was doing at the time. I wonder—did I keep my head in a giant bow-and-veal-thingy too? Is my head so very large?" and here she tried to measure her head with her hands, her set down teacup and saucer sinking into the sand where they had come from. She noticed this much too late. "Oh! My tea!" she wailed, attempting to dig after it.

"It is long gone now, my dear," the queen said. "But there will always be time for tea later." She brushed the ragged cat down off of her lap and set her cup and saucer down as well before standing and dusting—or rather—*sanding* off.

"Georgie, as usual, thank you for a wonderful tea," she said.

"My pleasure, ma'am." And to Alice—"Ma'am. Do come back again, when you can."

"Oh," Alice began, standing as well. "I will try." Of course, she had no knowing how she would ever manage to return *any* place more than once—she thought she had not been successful at it once yet!

"Come along, Alice," the queen said. "It is time we were off."

"Where to now?"

"I have some business to see to, and you—I believe you do as well."

With these final words, the Queen of Spades led Alice across the desert land and soon they were back to the firmer forest ground. They cleared out of the trees in nearly no time and stepped onto a cobblestone road that forked off into two directions.

"Which way now?" Alice asked, and though more to herself the queen was kind enough to answer.

"I must go this way," she said, pointing to the street on the left. "Which means that you must go that way—" And she pointed to the street heading to the right.

"Do you suppose we shall meet again, your majesty?" Alice said almost sadly. The queen observed this and smiled, cupping Alice's cheek in her lily hand.

"You may bet on it."

And with that gambling wager, the queen took her leave.

8. Rhat-psody

Alice knew that she ought to follow the queen's instructions and take the path before her, but she just did not feel quite ready to go on. There was an inviting pointed step at the apex of the two streets so Alice sat on it for a moment to ponder things. She had to ask herself— *What was the rush to get anywhere anyway?* Her thoughts then turned to the Queen of Clubs and this made Alice shudder. She hoped not to see her again anytime ever! She seemed the kind of person—that particular monarch—that your deepest nightmares were made of—the ones you never spoke of out loud.

"Ahem! Do excuse me, if you would—" came a tiny voice somewhere near Alice's feet. She looked all around to find the source of it, but there seemed to be nothing there.

"I am sorry, but I simply cannot find you—" she apologized, carefully lifting her shod feet to make sure she did not step on whatever had made the voice she'd heard.

"I am just here—you are very nearly sitting on me—"

Alice gasped and made to leap up, but the tiny voice shrieked.

"*Do not!*" And Alice froze. "Carefully now," it said in a careful voice. "Ever, *ever* so carefully—"

She carefully—as she'd been told—lifted her skirt and petticoat, showing to all the world her knickers, and slowly cracked her knees apart.

"A little more and the sun *will* shine in—" the voice said with hope. "And I *do* so need the sun's help right now."

At this, Alice folded herself nearly in half and found the creature in question: it was a rather large bug that had been speaking, and it was just at that very moment attempting to climb out of a most frightening looking brown shell shaped much like the thing itself. She stood slowly— still carefully—and sat on the stones of the street to take a closer look. The shell seemed stuck to the stone, defying all gravity, and though the creature inside was making diligent efforts to climb out, the shell did not budge.

"If you don't mind my asking," Alice began softly, so as not to deafen it. "What are you? I'd dare say a butterfly, but your chrysalis has claws and legs on it so I know that cannot be correct."

"Indeed, my girl. I am—" and it gave a little struggle here. "Or will be—a cicada, once I've gotten free from my former self."

"Can I help?" she offered, though truly Alice did not know what help she really could give, but she very much wanted to see the little—or rather—large bug, for she had never heard of or seen such a thing.

"Thank you, no. I was born to do this and I—am—doing—it!" and as sure as a cicada can cicade, it was at last climbing along side of itself.

"How beautifully you did that!" Alice praised, wondering how the now puffing-out insect had once fit inside the shell and more so—how it had squeezed out of the tiny hole so smoothly and perfectly without destroying it?

"Why thank you. How very sweet you are. Would you mind--?" It held a leg out to Alice and she put her hand down beside it.

"Oh! Certainly not, but—" and she slowly brought it up to her eyes. "You don't have those claws any longer—"

"No, no. And once I have dried out, I will have wings, just as our aforementioned friend the butterfly."

"And then what shall you do?" she asked in all eagerness.

"I shall—probably fly away. I have a concert to get to this very evening and I must be there by dusk."

"Oh. Will you be performing alone?"

"Heavens no! There will be many of us there. It is the one time of day that the frogs are good to the crickets and us cicadas—while we are making our merry melody, you see. They seem to enjoy chiming in and it distracts them from otherwise devouring us."

"That is most fortunate! So that sound that I hear near the pond at night—that is you?" she asked in amazed wonderment.

"But of course!" And Alice was certain she could see the bug smiling in gleeful flattery. "Well, it *will* be me and a few hundred friends. You see, it will be my debut performance and quite possibly my last."

"That hardly seems fair," said Alice. "Where have you been all this time?" she asked then. "Have you been practicing somewhere?"

"Why no, my dear. You see—I've just spent the last seventeen years underground."

Alice thought that an awfully long time to be any one place!

"Was it awfully dark?" she asked.

"Terribly."

"Was it frightening?"

"Perhaps to some, but really there is a lot to bump around on down there, the worms and other insects are rather polite. One really never has a moment to get lonely. It is once we get up here that it gets rather uncivilized."

"Oh." And she supposed the bug to be right about this.

"If you don't mind, I should like to be heading toward the pond. Do you know where it is?" the cicada asked Alice.

"Well, no. Not exactly."

"Oh. No worries then. If we start walking, I imagine we shall come upon it sooner or later. Were you readying to go, or—was I interrupting--?"

"Goodness, no," said Alice, and she stood with the cicada on her finger. "But I was told to take *this* path here, you see, and I don't know if there will be a pond along the way."

"Well, there is one way to find out, I say."

And in absolute agreement, Alice began along the pebbly road with her new companion.

"Do you have a name?" she asked it.

"Well, come to think of it, I've never really given it much thought. There isn't much need for names underground you know."

"Are you a—lady or a gentleman, I wonder?" To this, the insect chuckled.

"Why I am no ladybug!" Alice realized her mistake.

"Oh no, of course you're not! How silly of me."

"In plain and simple fact, I am playing in this concert tonight in hopes of attracting my lady love."

"Oh! Then certainly you are a gentleman!"

"*Gentleman.* I do like the sound of that. But no—I suppose I have no name. Could you give me one, do you suppose?"

"Hm." And here Alice had to do some serious contemplation. A long silent moment passed, during which time the cicada uncoiled its tongue and tapped it on Alice's finger. It only stung a slight bit like when she pricked herself with a pin, but it made her start nonetheless.

"Oo!"

"So sorry," the bug apologized. "Insect instinct, I suppose. I am terribly thirsty you see."

"Oh, yes, of course."

"What have you come up with so far, my dear?"

"Well let me see—I heard a story not too long ago about a dashing hero, who was not really looking for his lady love, but he happened to find her by accident--"

"Sounds intriguing. What was he called?"

"Well, I think his name was *Shellmerdine.*"

"Oh. Oh, yes, why I do like that very much!"

"Very well. Shellmerdine, it is."

It was then that Alice and Shellmerdine were happened upon, or very nearly ran into by a rather dirty looking woman in a very raggedy dress. She was scratching at her knotted up head of hair and muttering curses under her breath, and taking very little notice of Alice and her cicada. It took Alice only a moment to realize that the woman had a good abundance of mice in her hair and they were biting her!

"You have mice in your hair!" Alice exclaimed.

"Well of course I do, you silly girl," snapped the unkempt woman before continuing her ramblements, which now sounded to Alice a lot like *Thirty-six mice!* said over and over

"But why? Certainly they are less likely to bite you if they aren't in there, you know."

To this, the woman replied—quite proudly—" It gives me squeaky clean hair."

"That is just an expression," Alice argued, thinking the woman's hair to look far from clean.

To this came an indignant retort—"With hair such as yours, at such a length, I am *positive* that you yourself have had at least one case of the rats!"

"Well, yes—" She couldn't argue with that. Many times she had awaken with tangles that were treacherous to have combed out.

"See there! And anybody knows that mice are smaller than rats, therefore, I keep mice in mine."

"But—" Alice began.

"So—" said quite interruptingly. "As long as they are squeaking, it is squeaky clean."

"But—The squeaky wheel gets the grease, they say. " And to this, Shellmerdine nodded, having somewhere heard of such a thing his own self.

"So?"

"So, if your hair keeps squeaking, it is surely to get greasy eventually, and that is not very clean."

"You really don't know anything about anything, do you?"

"I suppose having mice in your hair would be better than bats. I have heard that if a bat flies into your hair, you have to have it cut out and that would be simply terrible!"

"I'm not talking about rats!"

"No, not rat—*bat*."

Really, what did it matter? Rats or bats—either would be bad to have anywhere near your head!

Rats and bats.

Alice sighed—not this argument again. When would she learn to keep her mouth shut about things that clearly were none of her business? She supposed never. Just then, the woman took off her *wig* and gave it a good shake. Baby mice went flying every-which-way, making Alice flinch. *The poor dears!* she thought. But before they could careen (--and Alice really did like the sound of this word and that is why she chose to think it just then) into anything, they sprouted tiny leaf-like wings and flew away.

"It gets heavy you know, them breeding in there like that."

"Yes, I imagine that it would," Alice muttered.

"You imagine too much," the woman accused. "That is your problem."

These words took Alice's tongue for a moment and she was not quite sure what to say.

"That is about the dumbest thing I've ever heard, I think," she mumbled, Shellmerdine nodding vehemently from her wrist where he had crawled up to. His tiny tongue stabbed at her again and she grimaced.

50

"My apologies," he said, but she hardly addressed it. "And you are certainly right, young lady, that is rather dumb. Let us not waste a single moment more here!" and he gave a flutter of his still damp wings, nearly toppling over, but Alice caught him—carefully, of course.

"Yes, I think it is time we ought to be going. Good day."

The woman only replaced her wig huffily and peered at Alice with black beady eyes as she walked by. The stare gave Alice a chill, the iciness of it reminding her of the Queen of Clubs and she hurried on until the woman was far behind them.

"Well, she was quite unpleasant," Shellmerdine stated.

"Yes, she was," she agreed without hesitation, before affording one more look back over her shoulder to be certain that they were not followed.

"Are you in the mood for a distraction, my dear girl?" Shellmerdine asked. "You look as though you might be able to use one right about now."

"Oh, positively, I am! Please—anything!"

"Very well. This is a little poem I composed. It is the very one that my concert shall be about tonight."

"Oh! That does sound intriguing, indeed."

The cicada cleared his tiny throat and began to recite:

"Morning—the death of night
As all who sleep now awake.
Promising warmth from the new sun
Against the blackness now shaken.
We arise with freshly opened hearts
And love of the truest we seek.
For only the bravest and the very bold
Of this gift ever shall peek.
So as the day is born of light and gold
And we rush to greet it with delight
It is not sadness we feel but gladness whilst
Mourning the death of night."

Alice greatly enjoyed his little poem and complimented him on it profusely.

"Of course, it has not nearly the same impact without the music to go along with it," Shellmerdine said. But still, it made Alice sigh dreamily.

51

"It makes me wish as though I were going to find my own true love. I wonder when that journey shall begin for me?"

"He'll find *you*, my dear and when he plays his song for you, you will know it and that he is the one. That is how it works."

"How ever did you come up with such a wonderful poem and how do you seem to be so very wise, never having been above ground before?" she wondered to him.

"That is what seventeen years of *imagining* will do for you." And Alice was certain that the little—rather, the *large* bug had winked at her just then.

"Will anyone be singing your words? During your concert?"

"No, but if any words *were* to be sung, it would most definitely be those very ones."

"I cannot play an instrument," Alice lamented.

"No? Well, it is never too late to learn, my dear."

"I can make no sense of it—the notes on paper. Rather, you may as well show me a page of Latin because I find it to make about as much sense." To this, she frowned deeply.

"I would not worry about it, if I were you. Your talents must lie elsewhere, whatever they are—we all have some kind or another, you know."

"Yes, I know."

They went on for a moment in pensive silence, the cicada the first to speak.

"You'd best take cover, my dear."

"I beg your pardon--?"

And at that precise moment, a spool of crimson thread knocked down on her head! She let out an indignant yelp and quickly ran for the cover of a gooseberry bush.

"Whatever could all this be about, I wonder?" she wondered, peering up at the sky through the bush's limbs. The sky had turned a nice shade of Kelly green and spools—and now thimbles, were falling every-which-way from it. They still made their way down on her, but the bush seemed to break their fall and the impact did not hurt so very much.

"A *sugar-shaker storm*," Shellmerdine suggested with a groan.

"A *what*?" she began, seeing nothing that even resembled any such thing. "Why that *is* the most ridiculous—" but she had to stop herself from continuing, watching the objects land, some bouncing on the ground, and then turning into small cylindrical boxes, the others into little gray animals that looked like some kind of rodent with strangely huge eyes, that immediately began to scurry about. "Oh *now* what--?"

At that moment, the cylinders burst open and jacks-in-the-box sprung out, each equipped with a rather large mallet in hand. At once, they began to pound as far as their springy arms and bodies would let them reach, trying to flatten the little furry things.

"*Oh no!*" Alice wailed. "What *are* those things? And why are the jacks-in-boxes trying to pound them into the ground like little fuzzy nails?"

"My guess is that they are sugar gliders."

"Sugar-what?"

"Gliders. They are native to Australia."

"But we're not in *Australia!*" It was a moot protest.

And just then, one landed close enough to Alice for her to reach out for it and she grabbed it just out from under the fall of a mallet. It was rather cute, and very soft—and it bit her quite hard! She gasped and quite by reflex, flung it away, the little thing getting malleted at once.

"Oh!" she groaned. "Let's get out of here!"

And she climbed out into the open, the falling objects having stopped, though the pounding went on around her feet. Where the sugar gliders had been, now there remained only little piles of white confection sugar.

"Oh, that is dreadful!" she wailed, as some of the powdered sugar got on her black shoes. "Why would something so terrible—even if the bugger *did* bite me, have to happen to those little things?"

"Where did you expect sugar so fine to come from?" Shellmerdine asked.

"Why, I suppose from bigger kinds of sugar, naturally."

"Oh, like a treacle-down effect."

"I suppose." But really, she didn't know, nor did she just at that moment care, but truly wished she could get the image of the jacks-in-boxes and their malleted victims from her head.

"Oh! I do so hope we are almost there," she said.

"I do concur, little one! I am parched!"

And at this point, the road began to narrow until it became only a muddy and very winding footpath and they began to hear the distinct sound of what Alice believed to be frogs, getting closer.

"We *are* getting closer!" Shell exclaimed. "I hear the peepers!"

"*Peepers*, did you say?"

"I most certainly did!"

"But, why--?" But her query left off there as she stepped into the clearing, the sun blindingly bright.

"*Eureka!*" the cicada hollered. "Mother pond!" he breathed excitedly.

But Alice could hardly see anything but the plentiful cattails directly in front of them, her eyes still adjusting.

"Looks as though we are none too early," Shellmerdine was saying, and by the position of the sun in the sky, Alice could only assume that it was some time shortly before—*sunset?*

At the vista of his beloved destination, Shellmerdine began to flutter his drying wings with anticipation.

"Should I set you anywhere--?" She began to ask, taking a few more of his little straw-like jabs with a sweetened grimace, knowing he did not mean to do it.

"Not yet! Round it just a bit! Please, just a little and a bit closer, if you could—"

And Alice went quickly, nearly to the pond's edge.

"*Not that close!*"

"Oh! I beg your pardon!"

"It's just that, the frogs are more kind for our symphony than on *most* nights, but still—"

"You don't want to take the chance?"

"Well—no. I want to meet my intended, before risking anything like certain death."

"Yes, of course."

And after a few moments' careful consideration, Alice set him on an oddly shaped, thin, gray log with a few of his kin. The log had a familiar shape to it but Alice simply could not bother with trying to identify it just then, the fascinating gathering before her taking a good most of her attention.

The little orchestra had a little conversation in their little cicada way, wings clicking a bit in a Morse code rhythm.

"Dear girl," Shellmerdine began, climbing up to her stockinged knee. She picked him up and brought the insect to eye level.

"Yes, dear bug?"

"Do, please stay and listen to our song," he said. "We shall be starting soon."

"Well, I guess I *could* stay for a *little* while. How long does it last?"

"Oh it could go on for simply hours and hours! But please—just stay for a short bit?"

And it wasn't as though Alice could think of a reason to have to hurry off just then, really. A few minutes certainly wouldn't hurt!

"Very well."

She set him—still carefully—back down with his new friendly rivals and found herself a thoroughly inspected and safe-to-sit-on, miniature boulder of a rock. She sat on it lightly at first, listening for any sort of shouting of well-hidden kings that may be lurking from underneath it. But as there were none, she made herself comfortable.

It did not take long for the cicadas to get to their wing-sawing, nor for the crickets to join in with their chirping and the frogs were soon at full croak. Alice closed her eyes at the steady and very cadenced noise and quickly fell into it as it grew louder and filled in every wave of space with a most pleasing though certainly sporadic hum. She could scarcely remember a single word that Shellmerdine had uttered to her in his little accompanying lyrical poem, but it did not matter—the rhapsodic symphony brought on the images he had spoken of, every sparking pixel of it quite personal and predictive of her future union. It was really quite much for her young mind to take and her eyes came instantly open.

"Would you say you were enjoying yourself, little one?" asked the gray log where Shellmerdine and his mates were deep in their song.

"It is loud, that is for certain," she began, "But rather ni—"

And she had thought the log to look familiar—as well it should have, for it was actually the Cheshire cat! He gave her a wink and his tail—now having softened from the wood it had once been, began to flap and swing haphazardly with disregard to the cicadas that were on his now back.

"I think it's nearly supper time," he stated. "Don't you think it is supper time, by now?"

And she could see quite clearly where his appetite was headed with this! His bristly tongue went to swipe one of the bugs from his back, but in only just the nick of time, Alice snatched it up and out of harm's way. The Cheshire's teeth snapped closed onto nothing but the night air, and Alice made to clear the rest of the bugs off of him before moving them to safety.

"Come on now—" he protested and Alice stood and began to walk away, drawing the cat along behind her. "You have confiscated my supper, you know!" he was lamenting.

But Alice was certain that she would not have been able to endure the sound of the crunching of the insect in the cat's teeth, no matter that besides—it just wouldn't have been bearable to see that kind of demise. The frog brunch had been quite enough already!

It really kind of reminded her however, of a time when she had been visiting with her grandparents for the summer. Her grandfather had loved to cater to her every little whim and childish want and often indulged her appetite for Boston Baked Beans. On one particular holiday, Alice had been outside on the veranda inspecting the vines that were climbing the trellis and she munched on the candied peanuts while her grandfather had his nose (and eyes) in the *Daily*. She really was the curious sort—inside and out of her head, and it was no surprising wonder that she was there poking around at just about everything, instead of minding her embroidery or other such lady-likenesses. It happened on this exact day that she came across a June bug—deader than a doornail, but a June bug nonetheless.

Its tiny little legs had already folded up tightly and all that remained of its lifeless self was a little maroon bean. She had picked it up gingerly and let it roll around in her hand under inquisitive observation before taking it to her grandfather.

Well, this was not *entirely* true. What she had done was take a handful of *Boston Baked Beans* to her grandfather, and he then promptly popped them into his mouth without looking at them. It was the act of a devilish little chit, what she did next—handing over the June bug to him—and though she had *only* intended to ask him what it was, she knew that he would not know the difference in feel from the corpse to the candy, and just as she knew she ought to say something (for he did not look up to identify this *new* little maroon thing in his palm either), he popped this too into his mouth!

It had been a most surprising little treat to him, and to Alice's great relief—one he had laughed through with dignity intact.

And this little tale, dear reader, Alice thought ought to be mentioned, for a story such as this could never have enough crawly creatures in it. Nor can we possibly let it be told from beginning to end without out dear Alice having something to eat, now can we?

Even if it is in but a memory.

9. Screaming and Dreaming

"**I** really think you should have let me eat them," said the Cheshire cat. "At least one."

"No," Alice disagreed.

"Why not? It wouldn't have been missed, most likely. It was really a tiny little thing." And he paused in their walk to hold two toes together as if to show the bug's measurements.

"Because, it wouldn't have been very good manners," explained Alice.

"Manners. Pssh. Who needs them?" the cat said flippantly.

"Why, *you* do!" Alice insisted.

"You could use a few yourself, little miss."

"I'm only a child," Alice excused. "That ought to account for something on my behalf."

"But you are a *clever* one. So you're not off of the hook—" and as the cat walked along side of her and said this, he formed his tail into a hook.

"Besides, he's going to lure his true love tonight."

"Is he now?" the cat asked, scarcely interested in the *how's* or the *why's* of it all. "Besides, it is not as though he is going to drop you a line now and then."

"You never know."

"*You* never know."

"The Queen of Spades certainly does have a lot of patience with you," Alice stated.

"The *Lovely* and I go back a ways, you know. Cats and single women—we are a goodly lot."

"How did you meet her?"

"I was a kitten then—quite fluffy if you can imagine."

"I can—I knew you like that once too, remember?"

"And she took one look at my *adorable* face and I reeled her in."

"Of course you did."

"Certainly so. It is factual," and he said this factually.

"Is it also factual," Alice began looking skyward, "that the sky is getting quite orange?"

"Indubitably."

"I am quite sure that I am not sure how I feel about that."

"What *are* you fishing at?" the Cheshire asked facetiously.

Strange things tended to fall from the sky when it turned strange colors, she remembered, and made for the cover of some trees that were in the loveliest bloom of periwinkle blossom. It seemed that the closer she got to them, the taller they got—or the shorter she became (it really didn't matter which), and even at the distance some of them were to her and the Cheshire, she could see that they were oddly shaped for trees.

"Why, they have figures in them!" she exclaimed. And indeed, the black trunks had human shapes to them, their arms curving up in a myriad of branches over their heads. "How *very* peculiar—"

"Oh brilliant," the Cheshire cat groaned.

"Whatever can you mean by your groaning?" she asked. "They are *lovely*! Why just look at them--"

And here Alice made a terrible blunder: She reached out and *touched* the ebony bark. It was beyond the cat to stop her and at nearly once, Alice realized her muddle. The tree above them lifted its human-like head and where a mouth would have been, the wood split open to resemble such an orifice—and it began to let out the most eardrum-shattering, skull-splitting, existence-piercing scream ever heard. The resonance stunned her, but having been through such a quandary once or twice before, the Cheshire knew only too well what to do.

"Silly girl," he said, but Alice could not hear him—could not hear *anything* above the deafening noise! He stuck his paw into one of her pockets and withdrew the seedling fluffs, stuffing one into each of her ears and sticking the third through one of his ears and oddly, drawing it part way out of the other. Alice did think it to look rather funny and now that she did not feel as though her head was going to explode, she laughed at the silly cat. He rolled his eyes and mouthed *simpleton* at her, for what was the use of speaking it out loud when he would not have been heard anyway. It was another minute before he pulled his stuffing out and motioned for her to do the same.

Silence met her ears.

"However did you get them to stop?" Alice asked.

"They tend to stop when they realize that no one is listening."

"How awful they must feel! Not having anyone to listen. How often do they do that?"

"Oh, every couple of decades, I imagine. And fortunately, that was about the extent of the length of any other ordeal."

"That cannot be good for them! I would think that only a few moments of screaming could not possibly make up for being silent for so many years!"

"Oh, trust me—they only need a few seconds. Anything more is gratuitous."

"How very strange," she breathed, looking up at the one they were still standing beneath. "I do wonder how they get *inside* of the trees, in the first place?"

"It is quite actually the *last* place that they get to," the Cheshire cat said, rather irritable about the whole thing, though he really did enjoy his ear-piping and only appeared surly for Alice's sake. His tail went up and he turned from her.

"Now, if you wouldn't mind, I have to go find something to snack on. And *don't touch them again!*"

And the cat began to wander off without her. Alice remained, her hands going to her hips indignantly. How dare he chastise her! All he would have had to say was: *Now, for future reference—touching the screaming trees awakens them and that would be kind of bad. Thank you very much, miss Alice. Now I shall be on my way.*

60

But really—whom was she kidding? She had tried once before at being a queen in that perplexing place and it really didn't get her anywhere then either. Why on earth—or wherever they happened to be—would it now?

"He can be a crass little bugger—don't let him make you angry—"

Alice gasped at the surprising new voice and whipped around to see a quite tall and quite attractive man standing there with her. He had the sweetest brown eyes and a boyish smile that was shining in them as well as upon his lips. And his voice had been pleasingly soothing to her, like sable brushing against her ears.

"Why, who are you?" she asked under the sway of his eyes, and seeing quite clearly who he was.

"I am the Sandman of course."

"But you look like the Jack of Diamonds," she stated.

"Yes, and you look like a little doll," he stated with a grin. "But I am *that* too", he said. "A jack."

"It is funny—I always pictured the Sandman differently."

"How did you picture me before, little Alice?"

"Well—" and she paused to think on it. "I don't recall, right now," she admitted, thinking him to look perfectly suited in his long, dark blue velvet jacket. "I suppose that I must be wrong about the Man in the Moon as well, however," she said out loud to herself, and then to him: "You don't by chance know the Queen of Diamonds, do you?"

"Of course. We are long-lost twins."

"Oh! Twins? How very lucky you are!" and Alice reflected that once or twice she had wished that she'd had a twin, though admittedly mostly for getting into mischief and having someone else to blamed for it.

"Yes, some do seem to think. We were born exactly eight years, eleven months and twenty-two days apart."

And this seemed most intriguing to Alice!

"Hm. I have not known too many sets of twins, but how exactly *do* twins get to be born so far—well, never mind." It didn't seem a tangality that she felt like untangling just then. "She is lovely, I think."

"That is she."

"Well, I met her not long ago today—or was it yesterday? By any matter—I was wondering—does she play the piano, do you know?"

"Why, yes. We both do."

The Sandman took one of Alice's hands then and looked at her fingers admiringly.

"I think you could too if you wished, though I think you better suited to play the harp." And here, he winked at her.

Alice decided that she rather enjoyed the Sandman's company.

"Shall we walk?" he asked her then. To this, Alice agreed and they began out of the Screaming Tree orchard, and their feet took them upon a sand-strewn road. This made Alice remember more of the Queen of Diamonds.

"Do you also do what she does? Dig in the sand for china cup pieces?"

"No. But I am most fond of building sand castles," he divulged with boyish excitement.

Alice smiled widely at this. She had seen many sandcastles only in pictures but imagined them to be great fun to make.

"You've never been to the sea, I would venture to bet," he said. And she wondered if he had been in her head earlier in this tale to have known that truth.

"No."

"But you have seen your share of sand," this he stated.

"Well, I suppose. So when my mother tells me that the *Sandman* will come to put sand in my eyes to make me sleepy, and that is why they itch so when I get tired—that is your doing?"

"Yes."

They took a few more steps, a large and fluffy bed set into the back of what was shaped like a seahorse coming into view. It was surrounded by trees dripping with pearls instead of leaves and so inviting did it look, Alice felt drawn toward it like a bee to honey. She did not wait for the Jack to come along before going directly to it and climbing into its meringue-like softness. It was divine and she melted into it, laying on her back and looking up to see that the Sandman was indeed there above her.

"You are feeling quite sleepy now, aren't you my dear?" he asked.

"Yes," but it was only a whispered confession. How could she feel sleepy, when she was nearly positive that she was already dreaming this? It seemed rather impossible, but then it was not—could not be. Not after nearly every last thing she had *already* witnessed there!

"It seems that most that I have come in contact with, have had either something to give or some kind of advice for me," she said thinly. "What do you have for me, my Sandman?"

And from somewhere behind his own eyes, the Sandman pulled the most beautiful, sparkling, peridot-green grains and sprinkled them adoringly down on Alice. She felt him hold her face in gentle hands once finished, as he brushed a kiss onto her cherry lips.

"Sweetest dreams, my precious Alice."

10. Pass the Scheme

Alice did feel that she slept most soundly—a dream within a dream, most likely and most naturally—with the help of the invaluable sand from the Jack of Diamonds. Was it any wonder then, that in the visions he evoked from within her mind that he too was a part of them?

She had been standing on the peridot-sandy shore of the sea in this dream, watching the foamy waves ebb and flow, the crashing of the waves sounding like the hollow roar she had once heard while holding her father's large conch shell to her ear. The Jack of Diamonds had joined her then, taking one of her hands in his and with a smile, led her along the coast, which was oddly intermittently bedecked with large white piles of snow. They exchanged no spoken words, and yet a zillion fleeting conversations at once as they went along, one such consisting something to the like of:

> *"Is that possible? To have snow on the beach?"*
> *"For at least one place on the world it is."*
> *"Where would that be?"*
> *"America."*
> *"Oh. It seems so strange."*
> *"It is a strange sort of place."*

And other such babble, and soon they stopped before an *en-gantic* drift-tree and they sat upon its white and weathered wood. The Sandman turned Alice's face to his, the rambling rigamarole of talk slowing to something more fathomable.

"Your sea, mistress," he said with a wink.

"It is so—" She had to pause to find a large enough word to describe it—"*Gi-normous.*"

"You have no idea."

Their sandy eyes grained together for a moment, before the tree beneath them gave out a low groan and ever slightly shifted. At once, Alice covered her ears with both hands, but this was not a tree after all and unlike the others she'd personally encountered, it was beyond screaming. They stood and stepped back from it, seeing rather that it was a giant squid that had been beached.

Alice gasped and ducked behind the Sandman for some kind of protection—though if you were to ask her, she would more than likely tell

64

you that she was not frightened in the least by this massive sinewy creature, but rather she'd been only slightly startled by the unexpectedness of its awakeness—and truly she needed no such service from the Jack or anyone.

"Come Alice," he said quietly. "It's nearing its passing."

Again with her hand held in his, Alice went to the drift-squid's great mouth to better hear what it had to say.

"Go on," the Sandman said to it.

"They'll come for me soon, they will," it said. This caused Alice to look at the Sandman for explanation.

"*Sand bunnies*," he whispered. Alice was certain that she had probably heard of *snow* bunnies, and as there was quite a bit of snow there, she didn't think it odd that perhaps there could be snow *and* sand bunnies about! And at the Sandman's words, the squid let out a very deep, rumbling and quite woeful sigh and whether it was from pain or helplessness or both, Alice could hardly tell.

"Come along, my little doll," he said, now leading her away from it. But Alice resisted, pulling against him.

"But, we can't leave it like that right now—" she protested. "All alone—"

"It will be alright. Things like that are taken care of by means that even I do not always understand."

And here (and she would tell you—very against her will!) Alice began to cry saddened, sea-salty tears.

"But—*why*? Why do *we* have to leave it alone?" She was asking the questions, but would she not have felt silly sticking around and hugging on a huge nearly deceased animal on its death beach? No, she decided—she would *not* feel that way!

"It's not, love. Look—"

And he turned Alice to look back at the squid, hundreds of white-winged sand bunnies cuddled up next to its great mass.

"What are they doing?" she asked, her tears forgotten at the near absurdity of the sight. Even he could only shrug at this.

"That is the magic of the sand I bring—you never know what dreams may come."

"Take us to something different, please," she requested.

He smiled and kissed her closed eyelids, whirling her off to the crow's nest of a great pirate ship. Far below them, was the scurrying crew, and whipping above them was their hoisted pennant. Alice could not tell what was on it, the wind made it flap so wildly, but it made no matter, a much greater view taking her gaze.

65

Along side of the pitching ship, was an arching and swimming, violet-scaled serpent. The Sandman saw what Alice was looking at and with a smile, pointed out several more of them traveling along side of the ship. It was immediately then that the wind ceased, but the tow of the currents that the serpents had made, pulled the vessel along with them, even faster than the sea itself could have mustered. The jump in speed jolted Alice, but she only stumbled back against the Jack and there she remained in cozy, close safeness. It was a rapidly moving and rapidly ending jaunt, the day expediently rushing into night as though they had traveled half way around the world! The halt came just as unexpectedly to Alice, but the Sandman's arms still held her and his stance was sea-fairing, indeed.

A tremendous hush fell over all, the serpents having silenced their *essing* in the waves and the waves seemed to stop waving as well. The Sandman led Alice down from the crow's nest by way of a glittering slide that had her landing in a ruffled flump at its bottom, his ever-present grin assisting in his lifting her to her feet. They crossed the gangplank and stepped down from it onto the back of a very stationary and scaled surface. A fluffy cushion had been placed there for them to sit on, the aqua blue velvet crushing silently as they took their place upon it. The Sandman pulled her close and handed her a brass spyglass, before nodding at the blackened sky, which quite at once began to separate into a fluid and oozing host of hues overhead. She looked through the telescope and they seemed to swirl together—expanding, contracting, weaving in and out of the patterned sky. Alice looked at her companion in question—*what does that?* She asked without asking.

Aurora Borealis

Aurora Borealis. The words went around and around in her head, like the colors went around and around in the sky. *Borealis—Bore-Alice—Auror-Alice Bore-Alice—*

And as the colors metamorphosed in the blackness of the sky, so did the words echo and shift in her mind, the sleepiness drawing her in more deeply, her sinking in against the Sandman sleepily deepening the drawing of her. But so comfortable it was, so sweet and inviting and meringue-like—Alice could not help herself—

Bore-Alice

Chalice

Malice

Palice

Talice-man...

And she felt she must have spoken here:

66

"I am part of such a great number of things!"

Then there were church bells in the distance, tolling and rolling and clanging and banging until quite suddenly, she felt as though they were in her very head! But of course, this was not so, rather, it was the Cheshire cat tapping on her forehead with his paw and she came positively awake!

"What *are* you babbling about, my little brook?" he asked her, hanging off of the seahorse bed's seahorse head. It took but a moment for her to realize that the Sandman was not there and as she sat up with a start, she began to search through her pockets. They were empty—even the red razor ribbon from the Queen of Clubs was gone.

"Whatever is it that you are looking for?"

"What did the Sandman give me? It seems that every time I come to meet one of the royal subjects, they give something to me."

The Cheshire clearly and dramatically smirked at this.

"Oh, you won't find it in there. Come on."

After a moment, Alice climbed down from the bed and followed the cat, the pearls hanging from the trees making the most pleasing clickling and rasting kind of sound as she pushed through them like the branches of a weeping willow. They had not gone far before a falling, glinting of gold caught Alice's eye and nearly clocked her in the head. Of course, like most small and curious creatures, she was straight away drawn to it and picked it up.

"Oh!" she exclaimed. "This must be it! He must have left this for me—"

"Oh, here we go—" the cat started, his warning speech brewing up in the galley of his cat brain. But she was already looking through it.

It was a highly polished spyglass just like the one she had dreamed of dreaming about using—or so she first believed. And promptly she changed her credence in such a thought. Rather, it was a kaleidoscope! The colors were vivid and plentiful and swirled around at the end of the metal tube just as they had in the sky half a dream ago. It made her smile and she quite enjoyed what she was looking at—until she realized that a piece of it was missing. She turned it around to peer through the other end of it, but there was nothing to see, and though it functioned quite nicely as it was, it was not in Alice's curious nature to leave well enough alone.

"I wonder what has happened to the other piece?" she questioned out loud.

"Perhaps a *serpent* ate it?" the Cheshire suggested jestingly.

"Of course one didn't, silly cat," she said, and here she began to look around the immediate area to see if perhaps it had fallen out.

"It didn't fall out," the cat said, sagely.

"How do you know?" she asked, only half paying attention to him, when her eyes fell on a small wooden box with a window in its lid.

"Oh! Perhaps it is in here—"

And sure enough, there was an oddly cut piece of clear glass inside, sitting patiently on burgundy velvet. She took it out, the edges well rounded so she did not fear an accident occurring from it, and without hesitation, she inserted it perfectly into the kaleidoscope.

"Oh yes! It *does* fit!"

"You shouldn't have done that," the Cheshire stated in his factual way.

"Why ever not? I have one much like it at home—"

"You certainly do not. Don't you know what that is? Well of course you wouldn't."

"Well what is it then?" she asked, looking at a climbing vine of blue morning glories as they crept up a tree trunk. The color of them was fantastic and she focused intensely on one blossom through the newly added clear glass of the scope.

"That is *Dora's Glass*."

"Well what harm is there in that? I am sure she probably misplaced it and I promise to put it back precisely where I found it in just—a—moment—"

And just at *that* moment, the morning glory began to grow very large and very quickly at that!

"See there?" the cat insisted.

"So?" Alice said. "I must be shrinking again. I think you would be most used to it by now. I know *I* certainly am—"

"If you are, then so is *everything* else and I do doubt that very much."

And Alice looked around to see that everything *did* remain the same size—except for the cerulean flower and its every twisting and twirling vines!

"*Oh bugger*—" she whispered, the scope falling out of her hand as she backed slowly away.

"Exactly," agreed the cat.

"What are we going to *do*?" she asked in a panic that was growing as quickly now as the flower itself!

"I would suggest running, but it seems that this is going to do us in and then what of it?" But running sounded, after all to Alice, a glorious idea!

However, thing was now the size of a small cottage and still growing, and the faster Alice and the cat ran, the faster the bloom seemed to grow after them! They were both very much out of breath and the flower was nearly the size of a cathedral before it stopped, and they stopped, and the white flakes began. They both looked up at the sky—which remained a passive pale blue—to see the snow gently falling down from a vast cloudlessness.

"Is-is it--?"

"Why, yes, I do believe it is."

And it was not long before the colossal morning glory began to turn a not so striking magenta, wither and then die. It was quite a relief to them both and the many living things that it must have crushed in its path!

Alice could not help sighing gratefully, as did the Cheshire cat (and if you have ever heard a cat sigh, it is rather amusing to be certain, no matter the circumstances!)

"That was a close catastrophe," the Cheshire commented. But Alice was already far away on the mesmerizing waves of her thoughts, a particularly sparkling and palm-sized flake having taken her interest now. It was perfect in every way, and so extremely defined that she could not recall ever having seen such a wonder! There was no leaving it alone, just as no child can resist reaching out to touch an iridescent bubble as it floats past them, within tiny tips' reach, though they know it is certain to pop if they do.

"How lovely!" she breathed, walking toward it in hopes of seeing it for as long as possible. It did not occur to her that the rest of the snow had stopped falling, nor that the closer she got to it, the larger it became, nor that something so fantastic could possibly be some kind of trap.

Which it was.

One hand's reach out to the snowflake and she was caught in it like in a sticky spider's web.

"Oh dear—"

"There now. *That* is a good one," the cat said of her befuddlement.

And the more she struggled to get out of it, the more she became fastly and molassasly caught in it! Within moments, she was hopelessly stuck, all arms and legs and a goodly amount of her hair, not to mention her skirt and pinafore and even the little ribbons on her pantalets.

"Could you lend me some assistance, perchance?" she asked the cat, adding to this-- "Please?" (Because one should always remember to say please!)

"Stop struggling so much," he offered, but something was not typical about this snowflake—or even this web, and why should it be? Alice stilled, awaiting further instruction, but none came then.

"I have got to find a way out of this," she said decidedly. "Any further advice for me *now*, cat, would be well appreciated."

"Take some of your own advice and get out as *quickly* as possible."

"Yes, but *how*?"

"Perhaps one ought to follow one's heart."

And to this, Alice thought about the small red heart that the Queen of Hearts had given her.

"Why, of course!" she exclaimed. "The little stone heart! But— I don't have it anymore. I think I've lost it somewhere along the way," she bemoaned.

"This, do you mean?" And the cat produced the very object of which she sought.

"Why did you not tell me that you had it?"

"You never asked after it."

And he took it to her, placing it in her bound hand's outstretched fingers, careful not to get stuck himself. She rubbed it between her fingers, feeling the smoothness grow unbearably hot and it dropped from her grasp. She gasped fearfully at this, but it was unnecessary, for the heart unfolded into a pair of searing hot scissors and set a reaction that melted through the ice. She was nearly relieved, until she realized that what remained behind and still kept her tightly trussed was crimson ribbon very much like the snippet the Queen of Clubs had given her.

"*Oh no*," she breathed, gasping when the ribbon began to cut deeply everywhere that it came into contact with her skin. The scarlet streaks began to grow and lengthen but they were not of the fibers, but rather Alice's blood, and there was a perilous amount of it!

Was there going to be a way out of this mess? She had to wonder. But she couldn't wonder just then, because the lacerations were biting and sharp and almost more than she could stand, and the blood— so *much* of it! And how sleepy and giddy it was making her!

"Alice—" the cat was saying from a short distance. She did not answer him, but instead giggled, the movement of the delirious mirth sawing her against the bindings even more.

ALICE

And, well, that was enough to bring her around just a bit—

"I never thought it was possible to be so sleepy without the Sand—" she was saying groggily.

"It's not, Alice—*you are going to die if you don't take this*—"

And the Cheshire held the china cup chip that the Queen of Diamonds had bestowed her with. But her hand seemed so far from his paw and it really didn't seem to matter much that she was drifting, drifting, drifting.

"I'll deal you one curiosity if you take this chip—" the Cheshire was saying. The very sound of the word—*curiosity* was enough of a jar to give Alice a little shaking up. For when had she ever passed up the chance for exposure to something odd?

"Well go on ahead then—hit me."

"It is said that most cats actually enjoy getting a bath. Especially if it is in a cup of clotted cream."

"They *do?*" Perked.

"Catch—" and he threw the chip at her, one bloody hand catching it cleanly. "Not really," he said. "Except perhaps for the cream bit—that is just a ridiculous and undermining proclivity. Now start cutting already!"

It was slow and steady, and very painful work, but soon Alice worked free her legs and arms, her weakened form collapsing in a rumpled mess on the ground near the Cheshire.

"I think *she* must be close by," he said, and Alice agreed, pulling herself up slowly and finding that the gashes were gaping

"You must do something about those, Alice," he said, before pawing a rather sizable sticky, slimy slug in her direction.

"What am I to do with *that?*" she said in repugnance.

"Rub it on them—they will stick closed."

Alice picked up the long, black, homeless snail using as little contact as possible with two fingers, and did as she'd been instructed—

--And here I must mention, dear reader, that this little event, was far more afflicting for the narrator to endure than it was for our darling little Alice--

The task worked wonderfully well, though once she was through with it, she had to hunt around for a moment to find something else to stick the thing to, as it rather liked sticking to *her*!

With a few rather deep sighs from them both, they traveled on for a minute or two in silence, the Cheshire piping up first.

"Do you think you have learned your lesson about going around and touching things yet?" And to this Alice stated:

"Probably not."

72

11. Rocking Horses and a Rockless Rook

Alice had to glance at the Cheshire to see if he was serious in asking such a question—but if she did not know better by now, why should he know better than to ask? He happened to look at her with a similar gaze, the questioning her own seriousness.

"Do you believe the Queen of Clubs is really near by?" Alice asked, her uneasiness coming back at such a thought.

"Only she could have set that trap—it had her mark all over it, and a marked card is a bad one."

Whether it had anything to do with it, Alice did not care, but staying away from the woman—that she would definitely try to do!

"I do so wish that the Sandman were here," she caught herself saying.

"This is not the time to get all dreamy, you know." But it wasn't just a kind of dreamy-ing, so much as it was a longing for his companionship.

It was very nearly too dark to see outside now, but there were a pair of monstrous figures in motion ahead and Alice quite decidedly dug her heels into the ground. The cat looked back at her from over his shoulder with a sparse raised brow and paused as well.

"You're not scared *now*, are you?" he asked. Alice hesitated, for truly she wasn't exactly *scared*, but after her last mishap, she had to ask herself if she really wished to rush headlong into any more traps.

"Well—"

"Come along, scaredy cat," he said. The words prompted her on, for Alice quite disagreed, after all she had seen and involved herself in, that she could be considered any kind of coward.

The moving figures before them turned out to be giant knightless horses from a chessboard, but they were on runners much like rocking chairs. Alice wondered at the size of the knights, considering that these horses were nearly five times her size! They were guarding a rook (that was easily five times *their* size) that was made of some kind of material not at all like stone. Alice did not know which to be fascinated by first! But the Cheshire spoke to the horses and her attention was reverted to them.

Of course, the Cheshire spoke to them in a series of indistinguishable meows and yowls and Alice certainly could not follow along. For a moment, it seemed that the horses could not either, for they took a very long time in answering. But then came another series of indistinguishable nays and extra rocks that she was certain were part of their answer, and behind this and them, there was a *swooshing* and *tinkling* sound that seemed to come from the lighter parts of the rook's structure. And following this came a sort of *zithery* and dull sound from the darker parts of the structure. She was on the verge of asking just what exactly the rook was made out of, and where the sounds were coming from, when the cat spoke, the rocking horses never stopping, only unvarying in their sway.

"Before you bother to ask, which I know that you will—the white part is *capiz* and the dark part is *operculum*."

"But what *are* those things—*capiz* and *operculum*?"

"You can ask the Sandman about them later."

And this was especially frustrating to Alice, for the Sandman clearly was not there for the asking and had she not just said only moments ago that she had wished that he were? But it really did not seem imperative at the moment, though Alice's curiosity was quite driving her mad about it, but more serious matters were at hand just then.

"*They*—" he began, indicating the rocking horses, "say that you are being followed and watched by *her*, and you should get into hiding at once," the Cheshire was saying.

"Which *her* are they talking about?" she had to ask, for she had run into many *hers* so far and some definitely warranted hiding from.

"You know the one. Go in there—" and he raised a ragged paw to the rook.

"But, what if *she* is in there? Do you think it safe?"

At this silly notion, the cat sighed a little impatiently.

"Rocking horses never lie," was all he said and pointed out the direction of the door through which Alice was to go.

She sighed as well and this called for a little nervousness, for what could possibly lay on the other side of that door? But that was only a far thought on the back burner of her mind, and she pushed against the slick and shiny white door. It parted like a curtain, making more of that *swooshing* and *tinkling* sound—and quite loudly as though announcing her arrival, at that—and she stepped into a large round room with a very high ceiling and no windows. It was not dark, but the several torches that lit it up, made dancing shadows all over the walls and it was a few moments before her eyes could adjust to it. She did turn back to the door to see if the Cheshire cat was coming along with her, but not only was he not there—the door wasn't any longer either.

74

"Come now, Alice," she was saying to herself. "You are much more plucky than you are letting on, so buck the pluck up a bit!"

And this little speech seemed to help enough to prompt her to a very large and very beautifully ornate sarcophagus lying in the middle of the room. She had to climb up onto a knee-high step that encircled it in order to look at its detail—onyx, carnelian and lapis lazuli encrusted into the gold to make the pharaoh's face on the tomb. It was very vast and very wide—too wide, in fact for her to even see all the way across, and she could not be certain, but it seemed that there was a dark hollow somewhere at its middle. As interesting as it was, and never mind that Alice had never before seen such a wondrous thing, she knew that she had to find a way out of there. Of course she knew that she was supposed to be *hiding*, but anyone who has played a very long and drawn out game of hide-and-seek knows that it can get rather boring when one is in their hiding place, waiting to be sought. And this was indeed the case for Alice! But it really was an interesting room, to say the least, looking nothing like she imagined the inside of a pyramid to look—though this clearly was no such thing, and what harm could there be in poking around? Perhaps she would find another door while exploring as she waited. After all—the door she had come through was gone, so if anyone were to come in after her, how would they get out?

She hopped down to the cold, hard floor, the echo of it resonating dustily, and then went to a scroll detailed brass music stand that stood in the corner by itself. There was of course a piece of parchment paper upon it, and to her delight, a riddle!

"Now we are getting somewhere," she said.

What is the only kind of letter never to be found in the alphabet?

"Let's see—" she began, thinking over the question, as this took some careful consideration. And as much as she hoped this riddle to actually have a real answer (for she had found that sometimes they did not!), she felt that it *must*, because not all riddles could be answerless, especially one in a place like this.

She had to read it again.

What is the only kind of letter never to be found in the alphabet?

And this brought her to recite her *A,B,C*'s at least three times— one of those times through she sang it—but alas! she could not think of an answer. She sighed and began to pace the room, the torchlight catching on something glowing somewhere near the ceiling and along the wall. The riddle was quickly forgotten as she ran to the very same part of the wall and looked up to see what could possibly have been making the light. Of course from here she could no longer see it, but above her was what appeared to be a desk mounted against the wall. Well! This was quite absurd and Alice knew that it was up to her to find out just what exactly a desk would be doing at such a place in a room—even if it was a room such as this very one!

The wall, upon closer inspection, seemed to be end-to-end shelving full of jars and bottles, which were in turn full of things or liquids. Nothing here was labeled, as the floating jars in the river had been, though what some of the things appeared to be, she was rather thankful that they were unnamed. She gently pushed a few jars back with her hands and found hand and foot holds. It took a few moments to get the hang of it, but she began to climb, scaling slowly and nearly to the ceiling, most careful not to slip. And she did quite well, becoming level with the desk. It had no chair with it, naturally, and she was unsure as to how it would have had any way to be suspended there in the first place, but she was able to get right next to it and see the blank parchment, ink well and quill that were on its top. The glowing that she had seen from below was in fact a small jar of gold blotting powder that looked quite unused.

"How very strange—" she began, picking it up while holding on with one hand. At the sight of the quill and ink, however, she got the notion to *write* down the alphabet, thinking that perhaps it would help in solving the riddle:

A B C D E F G H I G K L M N O P Q R S T U VW X Y Z

This, however, did not help much. She wrote them once more, getting quite frustrated with the entire ordeal and was just about to give up, when it occurred to her that one of the pieces of paper was not simply a piece of paper at all! It was an *envelope*!

"Why of course!" she exclaimed. "A *letter* that does not fit in the alphabet is one that goes into a *post box*!"

This gleeful discovery was quite interrupted when her foot slipped and she grasped with both hands at the shelving to keep from falling! While doing this, she blindly put her hand on the handle of a great urn and it toppled over! She gasped as a dark, warm and sticky liquid spilled out in great abundance, the smell of it reminding her of a stout port—or was it a *portly stout*? Whatever it was, it certainly did *pour*, right down on Alice's sorely pouting head! She tried to catch her breath, all the while not letting go, and shaking her head to clear the drenched tresses from her eyes, thankful that the urn had not fallen onto her crown. This was quite hastily thought, however, as it did begin to fall then, and to keep it from crashing down on her, she quite disastrously let go and fell far, far below.

Quite thankfully, Alice fell into the gaping hollow that she had suspected to be in the mid of the sarcophagus, landing in a very deep, rustling pile of small, square and very sticky pieces of paper. She went to pick one up and quickly saw that she need not bother, as they were stuck all over her, and the entire sarcophagus was quite full of this colorful little stickies. Alice soon discovered after holding one up into the flickering light that they were actually postage stamps. It seemed an ironic coincidence, considering the nature of the riddle and its answer, but she rather enjoyed looking at their bright pictures, most of them seeming to have birds on them—cuckoos and loons—in different sizes and postal rates. She got quite lost in them for a few moments, her remembrance of getting out of there coming back to mind. The opening that she had fallen through was at least another arm's length higher than she could reach, and it became clear to her at once that she was not going to get out the same way she had gotten in.

"But how *am* I going to get out?" she asked no one in particular. "I suppose it would just be silly to wait for the postman to come and get me out, for there are a great many stamps in here but no letters and what would be the point of him showing for letterless stamps? Oh, I shall never get out of here, I don't think," she grumbled. She groaned and sat down to think this through, all the while trying her very best not to pout about it. Surely there had to be a most simple way to get out of there! And then she would think of another most simple way back out of the rook itself! But this was going to take some sense, and she did not think that she felt the least bit *rich* just then. She would have to think of another time she had been in such a fix and then go from there. But the last fastened fix she had been in had been one she had nearly *not* gotten out of, had it not been for the Cheshire and her little trinkets from the queens, neither of whom were there to lend her a hand.

"Look Alice," she began. "What would your mother tell you?" And here she had to pretend to be herself. "Well, my mother would tell me something like—" And here she pretended to be her mother, talking to her pretended self. "*My dear, you can only go half way into somewhere before you are coming back out of it,*" and this seemed like solid wisdom, indeed! She believed that she must be at least half way into the sarcophagus—"So as I

77

cannot go back the way I came, I must have to get to the middle so I may get back out."

It seemed perfectly sound enough, and as there was no one there to pose any kind of argument with her, Alice began to dig down into the sea of stamps. It did not take long for her to hit the bottom of the sarcophagus and she was very nearly near tears when she suddenly felt the lip of a hollow vessel. It felt vaguely like a wide-mouthed vase or very large jar, but the coolness of the glass was unmistakable. She felt around its circumference, deciding that it was wide enough for her to climb into, and she did just that, trying not to think that there could possibly be anything unpleasant at the end or bottom of it.

"Please do not let me become stuck in this, or let it have an ending," she said to no one in particular, but hoped that someone might indeed be listening.

It turned out that someone had been listening, at least enough to warrant that her request was divinely granted, and she slipped through it with little struggle, the stuck stamps helping greatly. Only this landing was not as forgiving as it was into the postage pile—Alice landing on cold, hard stone just under the gaping mouth of a stone gargoyle, which was where she had been expelled forth from. The sky was dark and stormy and it was clearly night time now, and Alice was shivering even before she had time to assess her new whereabouts.

"Well, *you're* a fright for bored eyes."

12. Ti-ping the Scales

It wasn't as though Alice was uncertain about having heard a voice speaking to her—quite to the contrary, she *had*, but it took a moment for her to find the source of it, there in the near complete darkness. She had stood from where she'd landed, rubbing her backside a bit and began to look searchingly about without taking a step. But there in the damp, gray garden of stone that she was in, it was hard to miss the very large fuchsia orb-like flower that sat on a granite pedestal. It was plain to guess that the statement had come from within its papery folds but Alice went on to take apprehensive steps toward it.

"That's it, Alice, come closer," the woman's voice commanded, though not at all in an unpleasant tone. Alice obeyed.

"Y-yes, your majesty," she said nervously, though the Queen of Heart's body seemed nowhere to be found and she did seriously doubt that the matron had been changed into a pillar. This was of great consternation, for Alice did not much feel like having her head decapped again!

"She doesn't like you, you know," the queen said.

"Who?"

"You *know* who."

And Alice could only think of one *she* that the queen could possibly be speaking of just then, as she could not be speaking of herself.

"Quite actually," her grace of hearts went on, "She *hates* you."

"But, why?"

"Because, doll face—you are *you.*"

Alice could clearly see the queen's head and face through the petals of the bougainvillea now, her golden hair and gold-brown eyes glinting through, her head still looking as fresh as were it still attached to her body and the flower to its vine.

"Well, that," said the queen. "And your *kittens* infuriate her."

"*Kittens?*"

The head made a kind of nod at Alice and the girl saw that her pinafore and the dress beneath it seemed a little rounded out, of a sudden!

"You are having twins, you know and she does not like that—*not one bit.*"

"Twins? And kittens?" (Never mind that she thought herself far too young to fathom mothering either!) "Why would I not be having a litter rather than twins?" she caught herself asking.

"It seems to be the rage this year."

"But this is so out of order! Only this morning I was just a young girl!"

"But then, my dear—you are not so young as you are not so young as you once were, no matter how you try to believe it."

"I'm not?"

"Take a look—"

And Alice went to the still, silvery-black water of a non-running fountain and peered in. True enough, her once-child's face had transformed into that of a young woman and she did look quite grown up! But as exciting as this was, it greatly distressed her just the same.

"But what has happened to all of the years in between?"

"You lived them, my dear girl, do not fret about that."

"But however in all of the world did this happen?" she asked, not so distraught now, but somewhat fascinated. "And where did *these* come from?"

And she noticed the small, mewing kittens that were now quite suddenly cradled in her arms—one of all black, one all white.

"Why, the Sandman put them there, of course. Which happens to be another reason for her profound odium of you."

"I'm sure I don't know how you mean."

"Silly girl—you have been given something from the Sandman that she does not—even from any single one of her husbands, have. Dead or living."

And somehow with that, Alice knew exactly what the Queen of Hearts spoke of and it had nothing to do with offspring—quite actually— it was far greater than that!

The queen continued.

"You will need to remember this because she will try to destroy this. And do not trade him for anything she may offer you—*nothing*—no matter how tempting. Now here—put your children in those—" She nodded to a beautiful pair of podstakanniki, that had seemed to just appear on a similar pedestal. Alice did as instructed, first placing kisses on their tiny heads. "They will be safe until you can get back here." Alice felt a little concerned about just leaving the helpless kittens—her *children*—there, but somehow she knew the queen was to be trusted.

"She's not going to give up, you know," the queen went on. "Don't forget that. And don't play her riddle game, no matter what! I know how you can be enticed by them."

"Begging your pardon," Alice began humbly. "But how would you have known that of me?"

"It is so, Alice dear—only a riddle could have brought you here."

To this, Alice had to agree.

"Thank you, your majesty. For helping me. I don't know how I shall ever repay you."

"Oh, do not worry—you *will* repay me for it."

"I *will?*" And this made Alice a little uneasy and she could not help taking this a little indignantly, for she had not asked for the queen's assistance!

"Of course! You *shattered* one of my roses!"

"But I thought taking my head off was my payment for that."

"It was. But you have your head *now*, don't you?"

"Mostly."

"There, you see? Who do you think sewed it back on for you?"

Now this, Alice had not considered, but she was always one for pushing her luck just a bit farther.

"I did not ask to have it back," she dared. To her boldness, even the queen had to smirk with amusement.

"Dear girl—you *did* ask for it and I gave it to you. Now you must do the same for me."

With a moment's thought, Alice decided that she did think this rather fair. She supposed most people who lost their heads were not often fortunate enough to get them back!

"Alright," she agreed. "What do you want me to do?"

"You will have to go out of this garden and back into the forest. On the other side of it, you will find an open valley and containing a single tree bedecked with crimson blossoms. My body is being kept by two maidens and you will come upon them somewhere around there."

"Then what must I do?" Alice asked, already wondering what these maidens were like.

"Why you must bring it back here, of course!"

"Just like that? Is it possible that they will just give it to me?"

"Of course not. This life may be full of nothing but possibilities, but nothing in it is free."

"I shall try to remember that," Alice said, pondering over just what exactly she would have to exchange of the queen's corpse.

"Well, I am not being fair," the Queen of Hearts said then. "And after my little mishap I have vowed to go a little easier on everyone in every matter. *Almost* nothing is free."

"No, I suppose you are right, your highness—*as usual,*" she quickly added.

"Yes. Now get going. You don't have much time."

Rather, the *queen* did not have much time. Unbeknownst to her, even *Alice* had not gone much more than a day without her head, and it was well past that for the Queen of Hearts. She didn't feel that it would be very polite to keep the queen—rather her respective head and body—waiting too much longer, so Alice set about her way without further instruction.

Alice felt, as she ran from the cold stone garden, that she was being sent on a wild goose chase. She could not tell now how long she had been in that place, especially now that it was beginning to get light again, but there was no way an entire night could have passed already—*could it?* It was useless to even try to keep track of time—after all, she had presumably grown up somewhen—and she quickly set her mind to thinking about something else.

Still, she had postage stamps stuck to her here and there, though the liquor that had drenched her was now dried. It had stained her pinafore in a spattered pattern, but somehow she didn't feel terribly concerned over this or of what her mother would think of it—being one herself now. She supposed it was one of the many things she would now take in stride. Alice began to pick the stamps off as she walked along the winding garden path, sticking them into her empty pockets, thinking that it went on for a very long while of nothing but stone statues and pillars with nothing moving or breathing and it may as well as have been a graveyard, as lively as it was! It helped some, the sun coming up from what she presumed to be the east—though one could never be too certain of even which direction was which! And as the light of day began to illuminate all it touched, Alice dared to think to herself that it looked to be quite a normal day for a change!

Of course this was not to be so.

The trip through the forest was a short one, but no sooner had Alice gotten to the other side did she step into a ready-to-harvest vineyard, that appeared to go on for a long distance. But of course this was no ordinary vineyard: in place of grapes were bright pink and very plump starfish. She didn't bother to question why they were there instead of the usual fruit, but rather she wondered what starfish wine tasted like. She dared not touch them, trying to keep her task at hand also at the forefront of her mind. But as she went along, she noticed that their color was getting paler—or rather—they were getting *frostier*. She passed a few more bushes, seeing as she went along that the leaves and vines were beginning to become frost-tipped as well. Alice froze in her tracks—an entire row before her now covered in ice.

"*Oh no*—" she whispered, afraid that the Queen of Clubs was near by.

"*Guten tag.*"

Alice nearly jumped out of her very skin at the voice and the young man that was suddenly there with it. He had short silvery-blonde hair that was standing on end in very sharp little peaks, and he was dressed in silver satin. Two black spades were on the front of his jacket.

"Oh, did I startle you?" he asked, his breath freezing on the air though it was easily warm enough out of doors for it not to. Alice said nothing, but was relieved that he was not the queen. He extended his hand to her and she shook it, the lad taking it to his lips to kiss it and then bite it lightly. He grinned at her, a most mischievous tone taking to his brows. Alice's hand felt very cold from his touch and she put it in her pocket to warm it some.

"Sorry," he apologized. "*Frost bite*—" he attempted to humor her.

"Are you a Jack?" she asked.

"Why yes, I am," he said proudly. "Jack *Frost*, to be precise."

"Fitting. And of Spades?" she said hopefully.

"If you please." It was neither here nor there, Alice thought then.

"You're not the Queen of Clubs and that is what matters to me."

"Oh. No, I'm not her that is for certain. Why would you believe her close by?"

"The frost—she tried to trap me in a snowflake."

"Oh," he said with a guilty look but then the mischievous one returned. "That was me—I sent the snowflake to you."

Alice backed away from him then, bumping up against the vines and knocking a few starfish off of them.

"No, wait! Please—" Jack Frost said, reaching out to her but not touching her, her apprehension quite clear to him. "I sent the snow—not the web—they must have merged together." Alice felt chilled to her very bones.

"How did you know about the web?" She asked, nearly plowing backward through a row of vines.

"Everyone knows she sets those—they're her trademark."

He grinned again.

"I think you are fascinating, Alice, why ever would you think I would try to harm you?" Alice still was not comforted by any of it and Jack Frost could see this.

"Please, let me make amends—" he said, digging into his pocket. He produced a small wooden box that was decorated red or blue like the backs of playing cards on two sides, and a black and red checkerboard was on the other two.

"This is very special," he began, sliding one side of it off. "You see?" Inside was a three-sided block with the Queen of Spades on it. He turned it slowly to show her that each side had a different expression on it—happy, sad, angry. "All four of the queens are in here—one on each side, and you turn it here—" and he turned it from the knob on the box's small end.

Alice had to admit that she found the little box intriguing and very much wanted to take a closer look at it! This was more than apparent to Jack Frost.

"Do you want it?" he asked. Alice was skeptical about answering that. "Here—" and he took her hand to place the box in it. "Take it, it's yours."

"Thank you," Alice said. It was a guarded sentiment, but Jack accepted it with another grin.

"Enjoy it."

"I think I will, thank you—"

It was then that they heard an enormous clatter of cawing and it was getting closer by the minute!

"Why that sounds like a murder of crows!" Alice exclaimed and she was quite proud to know that a gathering of crows was called a *murder*, and it made her sound very intelligent to say it! Besides, when else could the mention of *murder* ever be considered a good thing?

"Those are meerkats," Jack explained.

"A murder of meerkats?" and that just sounded silly to Alice!

But they saw them then—sixteen meerkats all dressed in little red boots, marching in rows of four like little soldiers. Now this *was* silly!

"Where are they going do you suppose?"

"Your guess may be better than mine—"

Wherever they were headed, Alice and Jack Frost could easily see that they had their little minds very focused on their quest and they made not even the slightest notice of their observers. But those little diligently trotting varmints were a good reminder to Alice that she had her own duty to focus on, and it was also at that moment that she could hear her name being called in the distance—it was the Queen of Hearts' and my, how her voice could carry!

"If you would, sir, pardon me," Alice began, "I really must be going now."

"Certainly," he said to her relief. "I will see you again, I am sure."

She hurried off, making her way through the rest of the vineyard as quickly as possible, not letting the opportunity for delay to catch her and keep her there a moment longer! She did not quite know how to take this Jack Frost. As he seemed friendly enough, there was an air about him that put her on edge and she did not like it one bit! She did look back once to see if he followed, but he did not. Truth be told, he was merrily dancing about through the rows of starfish, tapping them here and there and freezing them under his touch.

Yes, Alice decided—there was something most disturbing about that little meeting. She would have to be certain to take care did the two of them meet again.

This did not harbor her thoughts for too long, for though the vineyard seemed unending, it did indeed end—rather abruptly—opening up into a valley, just as the Queen of Hearts had promised. There was a crimson-blossomed tree standing alone as well, just as she'd mentioned, but beside it was a very large pair of scales with a gentle and steady swaying to them. Alice stepped closer to see what was in them: the queen's headless body (though where the head would have been, a nice bouquet of begonias was instead placed) was on the left, and a pale-skinned and very pretty young woman with almond-shaped green eyes and who was dressed in red and white oriental silk was in the other. She was grasping on to the bar over her head, nearly hanging from it. She saw Alice at once and smiled most sweetly at her.

"Well! As I live and breathe!" she exclaimed excitedly. "We were wondering when you were going to come this way!"

Alice looked about, wondering whom *we* consisted of. She hoped the woman wasn't referring to the corpse! There was no time to consider this, for the woman began to holler for her companion.

"Molly!" she shouted, still smiling brightly. "We have company! She is here, finally!"

"I do beg your pardon," Alice said, "but, it seems that no one else is about, except for—" and she indicated the decapitated, flower-adorned body, but the woman kept smiling.

"Oh, my twin sister is here."

More twins? Alice thought. This was quite odd and captivating to say the very least! But still, she did not see anyone else.

"Molly—"

"Give us a hand here—" said another voice, though it was somewhat muffled.

"Go on then," the other instructed, having a firm hold on the bar above her head. At that moment, the woman's skirt lifted and another smiling, albeit upside-down and identical face appeared to Alice! This was truly a sight to behold!

"Well, hello to you!" said the newly appeared woman.

It was clear to Alice that these *twins* must be Siamese, though where their point of adjoining was, she was not certain. They seemed very much to her like one of her topsy-turvy dolls, sharing one dress that was actually two, and having to use their hands and arms as feet and legs, for they had none of the latter. Alice felt her thoughts becoming quite befuddled at this!

"Any chance of a switch, Olivia?" Molly asked her sister.

"Oh yes, of course."

"How—if I may ask," asked Alice, "Will you manage such a—*switch?*"

"Why it's easy—" Olivia began. "You just fold yourself like this and pull one end through the middle, like so!"

And here the two of them exchanged places, Molly now right side up and Olivia upside-down. Alice was positive that she had watched the trade, but could not rightly repeat in words just how it was done!

"You remind me so very much of *fattigmand* cookies when you do that!" Alice said, wondering if they knew what *fattigmand* cookies were.

"Oh! We get that *all* the time!" Olivia was saying, so confirming that they did know!

"Whew!" Molly breathed with relief. "One certainly does get used to the hand-stand, but *holey moley*, it does make the blood rush so!" She took a look around her surroundings then, noticing even before Alice did, that the grassy terrain around them was a bit dug up. "Holey moley, indeed!" she said then.

"Don't you mean *holy moly*?" her sister asked, as though Olivia could see the very spelling for the context in which Molly used the phrase.

"Precisely—*holey moley*—which is the same as making mountains out of molehills I suspect. And this very valley is superbly full of them!"

"Oh, then I am sure you mean *wholly*, Molly."

"Oh now you're just being silly," Molly said, good-naturedly. And then to Alice—"So my dear, what may we do for you?"

"Well, actually, I have come for—" and she paused, unsure as how to address the queen's partial self. But Molly saw where her eyes went and she understood at once.

"Oh—" she breathed in understanding. "How is her royal highness?" she asked politely.

"The queen is doing well, but she seems in a great hurry to get herself back together."

"I see." And she held the skirt of her blue and gold dress up so Olivia could see as well.

"But," Alice continued. "I don't have much really to offer you for it. Or rather—*her*."

"Oh." The conjoined twins exchanged a pondering glance and then smiled back at Alice.

"You may take it," Olivia said and this was enlightening to Alice!

"Yes," Molly agreed. "But in return, you must tell us a story."

"Just a story?" Alice asked.

"Well, it must be a heavy enough one," Molly explained. "It will have to take the place of Her Majesty, you know."

"Oh! So your scales don't tip!" Alice understood. "Well, I shall have to think about that for a moment or two." And she began to pace from one scale to the other.

"I don't suppose telling you about the time I talked my mother into letting me help her to make a pound cake would count, would it?" Alice asked.

"Sounds intriguing," Olivia said.

"Yes," Molly agreed. "I think I'd like to hear this one."

"Well, you see—a pound cake takes about one pound of each of its ingredients and that would actually make it a about a *five* pound cake. Of course, the day that my mother and I decided to do this, we were out of eggs, so I had to take a trip to our neighbor's to borrow some. When I was asked how many I would need I had to reply '*Six, if you please*'. And to this, I was told: '*Miss Alice—did you know that it takes two and one half days for a chicken to lay an egg?*' I had never heard of such a thing before, but it was true, I was told!"

"So did you get the eggs?" Olivia asked.

"Yes, and I returned home with them. My mother was busy mending a dress for one of my sisters and told me to put the eggs on the table and to be certain that we had sugar. Well, I can tell you—we did not! So back to our neighbor's I was sent to borrow the sugar. *'Miss Alice'*—he said to me. *'Did you know that it takes three weeks for sugar to get here from where it is grown?'* Well, of course I didn't know this—but I *do* know that powdered sugar is made a tad more quickly around here!" she boasted, the twins giving one another a knowing wink.

"So did you get the sugar?" Moll asked this time.

"Yes. But when I took it to my mother—who was now fixing my other sister's bonnet—she told me to check and be sure that we had enough flour—"

"And did you?"

"Not exactly. Back to the neighbor's I went. *'Miss Alice'* he said to me when I got there, *'Did you know that it takes five months for flour to be made from the point of sowing to the point of harvest to the grinding that makes the flour?'* I did not know this either."

"So did you get the flour?" (Olivia).

"Of course! But when I got home, I was to find that we were also out of butter and had yet again to go visit with our neighbor. *'Miss Alice, did you know that it takes about three years for Cheshire cheese to age properly?'* I was asked. *'No'* I'd said. *'But I'm not asking for Cheshire cheese, Reverend, I need a pound of butter this time.'* *'Well, it does.'* And when he leaned close to me with a smile he said *'Lucky for you, churning butter does not take nearly that long!'* Well, I was plenty relieved for that!" Alice proclaimed in all honesty.

"So you got the butter," Molly stated.

"I did. And before I left he said to me: *'Miss Alice, in the time it has taken you to go back and forth for the ingredients for your pound cake, I could have baked one for you and we would now be getting ready for tea!'*" Alice paused. "So I took my butter and my neighbor and we went back home and he helped us to make the cake. We renamed it the *Five Month, Three Week, Two and One Half Day Old, Five-Pound Pound Cake.* Fortunately, it did not taste nearly that old, though I do wonder now how it would have been had we put Cheshire cheese in it."

This required no commentary, but the Siamese twins silently consulted one another over it, as twins often are able to do. They took a long moment before reacting to Alice's story, but Molly was smiling and her eyes were sparkling emerald bright.

"Well, Moll, what do you think?" Olivia asked her twin while looking up at her and Molly looking down. "Will it do?"

"It certainly had a lot of *wait* to it."

"That it did."

"I say—" and Olivia did pause for a very long second, and Alice awaited her answer as patiently as possible. "Giver her to her."

Alice sighed, quite relieved, and not at all aware that she'd been holding it so deeply in.

"Yes. I think her story will be plenty heavy enough. Alice—" Alice came closer to the edge of the scale where the Siamese twins were. "Go ahead, dear. Step up on the scale and get her."

Alice went to the centerpiece of the scales and climbed up its shiny stem, climbing into the pan where the headless body lay in wait. She lifted one of the arms, the limb eerily warm and she thought perhaps she felt a pulse in the wrist. She dropped it before she could know for certain. It was silly to think that the body was living, but then again, it must still be or the queen would not want it! The tugging on her skirt by the body's raised hand confirmed that it was indeed most alive, and this sent Alice tumbling back in surprise and nearly out of the scale! The twins giggled behind her and she couldn't even afford them a glance, the tugging hand now snapping two fingers at Alice. She quite figured it poor manners to keep the queen waiting and she stood quickly, trying to scoop the body up from beneath the arms. It was hopeless—she could not get it to budge.

"I shall never be able to carry this back!" she wailed. "It is too heavy!"

"Take those—" Molly instructed, and Alice turned to see that the twin was pointing to something over Alice's head. She looked up to see two garters of gray goose feathers hanging overhead.

"Tie them—one on each of her arms," Molly instructed.

"They will help her go lightly through life," Olivia explained. "Or, back to the castle in this case."

Alice pulled them down carefully, seeing that they were just big enough to tie around the Queen of Hearts' arms and once she had done this—and after a short hesitation—she tried again to lift her. It was as though the body weighed no more than the feathers themselves and though she felt that she clumsily jumped to the ground with the living corpse, they landed safely and on their feet. She turned to the twins— seeing the scales still perfectly balanced.

"Thank you," she said humbly and quite pleased that it had all gone so surprisingly well.

"Of course!" the twins said together.

91

The firm tapping of the queen's finger on Alice's shoulder, followed by her arm being grasped and fiercely pulled on, brought Alice away.

"Do come back again sometime!" Molly and Olivia said simultaneously.

"Oh, yes, I will!" Alice called back to them, rushing along with the headless and hurrying body.

They were fast up the hill and running through the starfish vineyard, Alice wondering just how exactly did the body—which was clearly in the lead—know where to go? And why did it still have the begonias blooming from the neck? Alice felt a mild shudder shiver through her at that though—better that the flowers were there, she decided! But it was still terribly odd to say the least! She was certain that when she had been without *her* head, she had not been running amuck like this! Then again, the Queen of Hearts had been without her head for such a seemingly long time, she supposed that had she been in the queen's shoes, she would have made haste as well.

13. A Stamp for a Stitch

Alice and the living corpse made their way back to the stone garden where the bougainvillea and the frowning head awaited them. Alice was quite out of breath when the queen let go of her hand and made her way for her head, peeling the flower open carefully to lift out the smiling cranium.

"Well, my dear," she began. "You've managed it! And in a very goodly amount of time as well. Now come along—you've not quite finished with me."

And to this, Alice had to come along, for it had begun to rain globs of plum pudding and she was plenty much a mess already. She followed the queen out of the garden by a different path and to a house of cards that was amazingly withstanding the heavy pudding fall, and they entered through a round door that had been made of cork. There had been papers tacked to it, but they were in much too much of a hurry for Alice to stop to read any of them. Once inside, Alice paused to look around the place. It really did not look at all as she had imagined a house of cards to look on the inside, but rather it looked like a grand opera house with hundreds of red velvet seats lined up in rows from wall to wall. There were balconies overhead, a chandelier of what appeared to be silvery sardines glinting in the light and the ceiling was painted to look like more seats.

The queen was making her way to the stage, taking her head along and once she had reached down stage left, she turned expectantly to Alice.

"My dear, I haven't all day, you know, and neither do you."

"Oh!" said a startled Alice, and she dashed up to the queen, who was now handing her head to the girl before sitting in a nice little red velvet heap on the shiny hardwood stage. "But I don't have a needle—or thread—"

"Well I'm sure you can think of something to make do with, but get to it already!" and with this command, the queen pulled the begonias from their vase in her neck, revealing a grotesqueness of tissue and veins and things Alice didn't know much of nor did she care to see!

"I'll hold it once you position it," the queen offered. "But you have *got* to be quick about this!"

Alice obeyed, the queen's line of severage not so clean as her own had been. But then, had her head not *fallen* off? She imagined that to

93

be a lot messier than were it to have been *chopped* off. It was unnerving just the same. She got the queen's parts lined up as best as she could, wondering what she was supposed to use to keep them together and thinking perhaps that there must be a sewing room or wardrobe closet there somewhere, seeing as it was a theater of sorts. She began to rise, the queen's voice stopping her.

"Where *are* you going?"

"I must go find something to affix your—to your—"

"Just use what you have with you."

"But I haven't anything that would work—"

"*What is the only letter that does not fit in the alphabet?*" the queen riddled.

"One that goes in the post box, but—"

"*Yes!* So use what you've got in your pockets and send me on my way!"

At this, Alice stuck her hands into her pockets, feeling around and pulling out two little handfuls of postage stamps.

"Why of course!" she exclaimed.

"You can be bright when you want, can't you?" the queen backhandedly praised.

"I suppose I can," Alice agreed, setting the stamps out so she could see them. There were not too many—at least not enough for what she thought to be a thorough job of it, but perhaps enough to get by. Most of them were folded or creased from having been in her pockets, some discolored from having been drenched in the wine, but they would do. She licked them one by one and began to stick them onto the queen's throat, the stamps looking amazingly like hearts once they were stuck on, every last one having a little bird's head on it making quaint embellishments of them. Alice thought herself to do a very fine piece of work, as the queen rambled on and on about things, Alice only partway listening to her.

"Your *kittens* are safe and sound," she said and Alice's attention perked. "They are with someone who knows very well how to care for such dears."

Alice smiled, somehow knowing exactly of whom she was speaking.

"The Queen of Spades?" Alice asked.

"Why my dear, you *do* have some smarts, don't you?" This was a little stinging and Alice's smile darkened some.

"I do beg your pardon, your majesty," she began, "But whatever happened with your deciding to be kinder."

"Oh. You are right—I did say that, didn't I? Well then, *I apologize*. There now—that felt rather nice." Though the queen grimaced a slight bit at her admission.

"I suppose being kind does feel nicer than being cruel—" And Alice did know this from experience, having once (*or twice—alright, several times*) treated one of her sisters in a rather cruel way and remembering how terribly awful she had felt afterward.

But now really wasn't the time to be reminiscing about sibling nastinesses, for she was starting to feel a little dizzy in her head and wondered why there were now two Queens of Hearts before her. It made it rather difficult to finish affixing the stamps on her!

"I say—" the queen was saying. "Whatever is the matter with you?"

"Forgive me your majesty," Alice was beginning to say. "But I cannot figure which of you is you and which you to stick with this sticky sticker."

The queen, who was now nearly completely complete again, took hold of Alice's held out hand, the last postage stamp clinging to her fingertip like a little paper flag. Alice could not help herself and began to giggle uncontrollably. The queen peeled the stamp off and looked at it closely, seeing a few dark drops that had dried into its picture and determined that they had not been a part of the original design.

"Hm."

She raised it to her nose, smelling the alcohol on it at once, as Alice continued to laugh and laugh, falling down onto her bottom, her skirt and petticoat fluffing all about her in a rather unladylike way. The queen only smirked, somewhat amused.

"Why Alice—you are foxed," she stated, her hands on her hips as she stood, now feeling a lot more like her old self again.

"Am I?" the girl asked, but she only knew that the room was a sparkly blurry mural and the queen was a red and white—but mostly red—shapely spindle standing over her. Alice thought her to look very much like a sugar bowl with her hands on her hips like that, only perhaps not quite so round as one. This only brought on another fit of hysterics and the queen *tsk tsk'd* at her before tying the feather bobeeches around Alice's arms and then lifting her into her own.

"Where am we—I mean, where are I—oh bother!" and she giggled, putting her head against the queen's shoulder and thinking her to smell very much like freesia.

The queen took her across the stage and behind the scarlet and gold ruched velvet curtains to a piano bench. She opened the top of it and placed Alice into the bed of it, the many sheets of music feeling rather petal-soft to her just then.

"You shall be safe in here until you get abstemious again." And she plunked down the lid, leaving Alice in darkness. She really did not have time to think about where she was or how she was ever going to get out of there before she became aware that she was in company.

"Well, hello sweet Alice."

"Oh—Jack—" she said, feeling his face in the darkness. But she had met two Jacks now and she wondered which one he was. She hoped he was the *right* one, but then, there was not a titch of coldness there.

"Yes."

"Now how do I know this?" she asked, partly to herself.

There came a mouth-watering green glow then from his hand and he held it up so she could see his face. It was a most comfortable place to be, she felt, having her Sandman there with her.

"Are you here to go sailing with me again?" he asked, but her tummy was already pitching and rolling like the high seas.

"Oh, I cannot."

"Perhaps we can sail from more solid ground then," he suggested, blowing the glowing grains gently at her eyes. She had to close them, rubbing hard and then reopened them to find that they were no longer in the piano bench, but rather sitting on a dock with a steady flowing river passing below them. There was a pile of pale green colored sheet music between them and already the Sandman was folding a piece of it until he had created a small boat. He handed it to Alice, the black notes looking like sailors and the song's title was along the side where the little boat's name would rightfully be. She smiled, feeling dreamily comfortable and realizing this as he was folding another one.

"Shall we race them?" he asked her, finishing his second boat and making a third.

Alice picked up a piece of music and copied his folding, making one of her own, the song title lining the sail. The upside down-ness of it made her frown, but the Sandman smiled at her, and she handed it to him. He took it, looked it over and put it on as a hat instead, tipping one onto her crown as well.

"However does one read this?" she asked. "All these dots— these notes—how do you get them to make sense on the piano that you're playing?"

The Sandman picked up an unfolded sheet and as he tapped the notes on the page as he would the keys on the instrument, they sounded to her ears. This made Alice grin bright and bemusedly. He played a song for her then that sounded somehow familiar though she could not place it exactly. It was something she knew from very deep within and it was a song that she'd heard from no one but this very man. She felt there was no grasping what it was and just listened, while taking a swim in the molasses of his eyes. She heard the music continue and though she never looked away, she saw the two of them setting the paper boats adrift and they watched them float away on the milky-white water.

"*This is bliss*—" she heard herself say, her head resting on the Sandman's shoulder, his kiss landing on her head.

And it was bliss to be sure, whether from the stamps she had licked or from her Sandman's company, she couldn't tell and it didn't

97

matter. It was the sweetest place Alice could think of to be just then or any when ever.

"*I am sorry that I must leave you again soon,*" he was saying softly, but she felt him closer than ever before to her, as though their very existences were conjoined and would never separate. "*I will return though, my Alice. Always, I will be coming back for you—*"

She watched a few more boats float by, before turning her face against his chest and falling into the innermost heart of him...

It was as though someone had dropped the fallboard down over a piano's keys, the loud banging of it awakening Alice, and she opened her eyes to see that she was now beneath a tree just outside of the house of cards. The little river was gone, and the paper boats—and her Jack. Alice sighed and sat up, not liking her sudden aloneness. It was far too lonely and boring that way, she decided firmly. She went to shove her hands into her pockets for something to do with them, knocking the fingers of one hand right into the forgotten wooden box that had been given to her by Jack Frost. She pulled it out and inspected it carefully, no side indicating which particular queen was hiding behind which little sliding door. Alice turned it over a few times before sliding one side up. It revealed the Queen of Clubs and though Alice dreaded seeing the glowering face, she could not help turning the knob to see the woman smile and then frown in despair. She knew it wasn't right but Alice rather liked seeing the woman in the latter two expressions. She turned it back around and around, the knob only turning clockwise, so she had to pass the angry face each time. It quickly grew tiresome and she began to spin it faster, like a top inside of the box.

Well! *This*, Alice should not have done!

The box grew very hot in her hands and she dropped it, the landing from the little thing being so hard, that it made a very deep hole in the ground, which caused the terra under her feet to shake terribly! Alice stumbled about, trying to regain her balance, watching as the sky darkened to a frightening mixture of midnight and magenta and the foliage around her turned black and dead. A final hard shake and Alice found herself landing hard on her rear on what had once been the ground, and was now the unforgiving floor of a sickeningly, psychotically spinning carousel. It was pillared by the trapped forms of people—also black, slick with rot and seemingly dead, who were themselves spinning within their caging bars as if into eternity. Alice grew very frightened, very quickly and closed her eyes tightly, wishing for it to end, or for the spinning to stop at the very least!

It did stop then—quite abruptly, coming to a break-neck halt. She uncovered her eyes slowly, the forms inside of the cages now suspended limply against the bars. She stood and looked around, and though the entire structure was open like a carousel ought to be, there seemed no way off of it.

And then there was a black and looming shadow growing up over the structure, leaving Alice in the darkness of it. It got denser and more suffocating and began to take shape, until Alice realized that it was none other than the Queen of Clubs. The dread Alice had felt while looking at the queen's face in the puzzle box was a zillion fold now, especially at seeing that she was but a fraction of the queen's size, and there was no escaping her.

14. Unjust Desserts

"Well goodie," said the Queen of Clubs in a voice so booming and loud that Alice had to cover her ears with her hands against it. "Look what the cats have dragged in."

She opened the top of the carousel by knocking it off with one of her mirrors, the soulless black bodies in their cages only slightly rattled and unnoticing of the change.

"It is about time you came around, Alice," the queen was saying. "You have certainly taken your time about it."

"Your majesty—" Alice began a little timidly, certainly not wanting to be crushed by the woman and it was quite apparent that she could be! "I am so very small, I am afraid, that your voice is hard for me to understand clearly—" (Which was partly true and not really much of a fib.)

"Oh, you *are* a clever girl, aren't you," the queen said, but not so much as a compliment as it was an observation. But still, the queen did reduce herself to closer to Alice's size, though she remained as puffed out as she had been the day Alice had met her, and she still stood nearly twice as high as the girl.

"What do you want with me?" Alice asked, knowing fully well that she was captured for some very particular reason. "I assure you, your highness, I do not have much to give you."

"*Ipso facto*, my dear—you indeed *do!*"

"I-I *do?*" And *ipso facto*, Alice could not think of a single thing that she could offer her.

"Tell me—do you like to play games?"

"Why, yes, I do like most games," Alice admitted, cautiously.

"Fantastic! Let's play a game then!" And at the queen's excitement over this, Alice grew evermore wary.

"What kind of game?"

"It is a very easy one," the queen promised. "It is a *trading* kind of game."

"Trading game? I don't believe I've ever heard of one played quite like that."

"It is grand, really. For instance—what would you like more than anything right now?" and before Alice could answer, the queen answered for her—"To get off of this carousel, perhaps?"

"Well, yes, for starters, I would like to get off of this terrible thing!" Alice confessed.

"See? So the game has begun!"

"But, I didn't—" But it was too late: the queen was already playing.

"I can help you off, for I am an *excellent* trader, if you agree to *my* request."

"What *is* your request, your majesty?" Alice asked, not really wanting to know this, and she was very right in feeling thus! And to these—the very words the Queen of Clubs was hoping to hear, the woman answered:

"I'll let you off of this merrily-go-round—" And she offered this so casually, all the while swinging the mirrorless green ribbon around, that it made Alice's blood dizzy. She knew what was coming. "—If you tell me where your Jack is."

Alice felt her heart drop, but then it began to race painfully in her chest.

"No. I won't give him to you for that." And Alice truly could be a very stubborn little girl when she wanted to! To show this, she crossed her arms across her chest defiantly. Of course, it was more to keep her heart from beating right out of her very ribs, but the Queen of Clubs did not need to know this!

Her response clearly angered the queen, and though the woman's chalky-gray face went rather red, she still maintained a stiff smile, the ribbons no longer swirling around. It rather made Alice's stomach turn to think that the queen wanted to add him to her collection—had she not enough husbands already?

"Very well," the queen was saying. "You may go—"

At her words, a gate opened off of the side of the carousel and a path through an ominous looking garden appeared. Alice, not wanting to give the queen a chance to change her mind, raced for the gate and had one foot onto the dirt before the queen spoke, her words stopping her instantly.

"Of course, if you go that way, you'll be traveling through patched beds of belladonna, certainly foxglove, definitely monkshood, some sumac, the most stinging of nettles, a little hemlock, a bit of hogweed, maybe a spot of spotted jewelweed—all of which are highly lethal, and a good many of them deadly just by the mere touch of them. Why, even the soil is so poisonous, it is a wonder the plants can even grow! And really, you're not terribly likely to survive that. But by all means—*go ahead* and try if you like!"

At the glee with which these words were spoken, Alice thought it better to pull her foot back, and not take the garden's route.

"I *could* give you a few other options, you know," the queen was saying. "Far be it from me not to be *fair* about something like this, even though you really aren't being all that cooperative about it."

Alice ignored this statement, thinking it to be rather unfair in itself.

"What are your two other *options* for me then, your highness?"

"Well, you are welcome to have a piece of pie, if you would rather," she offered, pointing to a cloth-covered pie that had not been on the floor of the carousel a moment before. Alice hesitated, but the queen was smiling in a deceivingly sweet way. "I made it myself this morning—it is rather good. My own special recipe, you know."

Alice did go to it then, lifting the cloth slowly and finding a very simple crust-covered pie in a gold baking dish. It looked harmless enough. The queen approached her and handed Alice a very large golden spoon from between the bars.

"It's poisoned—" Alice stated, having taken the spoon skeptically.

"No! No poison, I promise you. Goodness, no! What a terrible waste that would be!"

If there was no poison in it, Alice thought, then what could be the harm? Yet, it seemed much too simple of a solution—and of course, she was right to think this!

Still, she pushed the spoon down into the flaky golden crust, an angry rumbling coming from within along with the rising up of purple juice, stopping her.

"Of course, it is a *bumble berry* pie," the queen said. And the source of the bumbling was becoming quite loud and furious now!

"I cannot eat this," Alice said softly, hoping that the very irate bees would stay put beneath the only thing that was separating them from her, very thin pastry as it was!

"Fine," the queen agreed. "I suppose, you will just have to answer my riddle then."

"A riddle?" Alice repeated. "That is all? Just a riddle?"

"Yes. You like riddles, don't you?"

"Well, yes, of course I do." And truly she did, despite her knowing better of it! "But that is all I must do? Answer it, and you will allow me to go free?"

"I will allow you to *go*, Alice. Yes. It really is a simple one," the queen bragged. "You'll be *gone* in no time at all! Ready?"

"Well," Alice began, knowing that the simplicity of it could not be just that, but what other choice did she have? "If that is all I must do—just answer the question, then I suppose, I must agree."

"Of course you must!" and the queen said this a little smirkingly, her outward moods changing like the ferocity of the sky above them. Really, Alice thought, at this point, what harm could there be in it? Certainly it could not be worse than her other proposed options. She gave a meek nod and the queen pounced all over it.

"Here we go then:

The maker doesn't want it, the buyer doesn't use it. The user never sees it."

Alice had to ponder this for a long moment, all the while the Queen of Clubs pacing around in front of her, repeatedly checking herself in her mirrors and sticking her fingers into her curls and huffing about impatiently.

"It must be *killing* you that you've not yet guessed the answer," she said, derailing Alice's train of thought. Of course, it was rather hard to concentrate on anything while watching the queen, as she was most distracting!

Alice thought on for a moment more, the queen holding the green ribbons that were clearly intended for the Sandman—*Alice's* Sandman—up in front of the girl.

"You'll absolutely *die* when you figure it out," the queen said with promise edging her haughty tone. Alice turned away from her to think.

"Let's see here—*The maker does not want it. The buyer does not use it. The user does not see it.*" Alice too began to pace, as it seemed to help the thinking process somewhat. (Really, you ought to try it for yourself sometime if you ever have the need for it!)

"A book of *Braille?*" she guessed then. "No—I suppose the user *would* actually see that, in a manner of speaking, at least with his hands. A *birdhouse*? No, the birds would see that as well."

"You're *digging* in the right direction—"

"Digging?"

The thoughts continued to swirl and then it came to her:

"A—*coffin?*" she uttered mostly to herself. "Well, that would make perfect sense! Yes, of course! The answer is *a coffin*—" And as soon as the words crossed her lips, Alice knew she should not have spoken them!

"Correct! And silly Alice—you really should know better than to trust things around here that make any kind of *sense!* You should know by now that we don't have that sort of thing around here. On the other hand—*You do win!*"

And before Alice could think anything of what was happening, the floor beneath her feet began to shift, the sectioned panels moving quickly and rearranging until a small, tight structure was walling up around her! She scarcely saw what it looked like but it was slightly dome-like and Alice feared that it might be shaped somewhat like a beehive! It was swiftly closing around her, and when there was but a crack left, she saw the Queen of Clubs approaching with the pie and a very smug sneer.

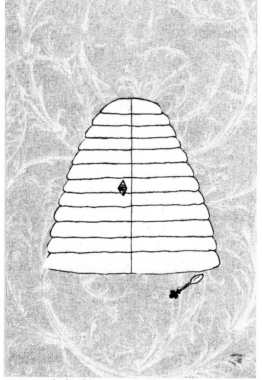

"But, you can't do this to me!" Alice cried—or at least attempted to.

"Stupid Alice! Of course I can!" the queen spat. "Did you not hear me say that it was a *trait- ing* kind of game? I *told* you that I was a excellent *traitor!*" And she stuck her face close to Alice's. "Don't you feel even a little betrayed?"

"Very much so—" Alice whispered, feeling her scorching hot tears running down her cheeks. She wanted very much to wipe them away but truthfully, she was now too petrified to move. This did not stop the queen. It did not sway her even the tiniest bit.

Without further ado, the queen shoved the pie in with Alice, and it clattered to the floor as the coffin-hive shut up tightly and completely, the infuriated bees flying free from the pan and swarming up around her. There was barely any room to struggle but Alice's panic was enough to incense them further and the burning stinging came a *buzzillion* times!

Now, dear reader, you must be wondering just how exactly little Alice could possibly survive this! The truth is…well, actually, she did!

Alice was not allergic to bees and even though these were honeybees and their sting should have been tragic at such a high rate, the flour and berry juice from the queen's pie created a kind of paste and immediately drew the venom directly back out.

It took a few long moments for Alice to convince herself to stay calm and to stop swiping at the bees, as it only made them madder, and once she had settled enough to take a look around, she realized that there was a small opening just large enough to peep through at knee level. It was rather hard to crouch down to take a look, but she somehow managed it and she could not believe what she saw!

It was as though a billow of green mist was heading across the dismal scape, and before the Queen of Clubs could react, the mist solidified. Face to face, stood the Queen of Clubs and the Queen of Diamonds, the first looking rather surprised, as the other looked quite displeased. The Queen of Diamonds spotted the hive then and rushed to it, Alice seeing the soft celery silk of her dress as it brushed up against the tiny opening. The queen turned away at once, leaving a gentle trail of jasmine essence in her wake.

"*You!*" she said to the other queen. "*You were the one that got into my apiary!*"

"Yes," the Queen of Clubs admitted. "I took them all, your precious little bees!"

"*And the girl. She is in there too, stationary.*"

"Yes," the queen said flippantly.

"*You must give them all back!*" the Queen of Diamonds demanded.

"No." This she also said with little regard. "Unless of course, *you* would like to ante up for them."

"*You gorgon, I am not the keeper of that Jack!*"

105

"Suit yourself, then—she can die, for I care not. She is nothing to me and you are little more than that."

Alice could plainly see that the Queen of Diamonds was getting rather furious herself and was not taking the Queen of Clubs or her words kindly. Yet she was rather impressed that the woman continued to speak in rhyme, and despite her own predicament, Alice had to smile at that!

"Too much trouble you cause with all of your frivolous malice—" she said, looking more beautiful in her strength and unyielding poise. But then she turned to the hive and caught Alice's eyes with her own, the look in them quite sad.

"I am most sorry, my darling Alice—"

Before Alice could interpret whatever the queen could mean by such words, the floor beneath her dropped out and she fell through blackness for a long, long while—a falling unlike any other that she had ever endured—before finally landing in a room with nothing but a table, a mirror and a single flickering-flamed candle.

15. W.A.R. (Warranted Antipodal Reunion)

*Y*ou are probably wondering what was to happen next to little Alice, as surely she was thinking that very thing! And because what happened next between the Queen of Diamonds and the Queen of Clubs was something that our dear Alice would certainly not want to miss, I will tell you how she managed it!

The small room she found herself in had no doors, no windows and otherwise no way in or out. It really did not matter how she got into it in the first place—her only care was getting out of it! She looked over the table, and then under it, finding nothing but the candle with its golden flame. She then picked up the candle and inspected it as well, careful not to spill any of its hot ivory wax. At last, she went to the mirror and took a long hard look into it. There was quite obviously her reflection staring back at her, stitches fully gone and wound healed—even the raised pink bee stings were leveling off rather quickly. She did appear a little older to herself and certainly she was a filthy ragged mess, but that was the least of her matters. She did know, that despite all of these things that were somewhat logical at the time, it seemed that getting out was going to be altogether *illogical*. How much more perfect could that be, she thought, considering that it was making sense that got her there in the first place—why should it not be nonsense that got her *out* again?

Alice had to stop this thinking, for it was not getting her anywhere! Instead, she gazed back into the mirror, seeing what she saw. She then took the saw and went to the table, first removing the candle and then cut it into two halves. Now Alice, having some smarts as the Queen of Hearts had earlier praised her, knew very well that two halves make a whole. And a *hole* was just what she needed! It was a tight squeeze, but on her belly and with the lit candle in hand, Alice went through the hole, hoping as she crawled through it, that it did not have a cul-de-sac or an otherwise perturbed animal at its other end! This was not to be so, however, and quite uneventfully, Alice inched her way free.

She was awaited at the other end and held down onto the pebbly ground by the Queen of Spades, who seemed to have not a single qualm what so ever about laying on the dirt and otherwise getting her beautiful lace rather mussed. The Cheshire was right along with her, but felt more at home standing on Alice's back.

"Stay down here," the queen whispered to Alice. "You're supposed to be quite buried!"

It certainly was shocking enough to Alice that she had ended up outside, much less with the Queen of Spades there with her, but then to have the Cheshire cat climbing up on top of her with the exact sort of nonchalance expected of him—it really was a surprise to Alice all the same!

"Hello lovey," he said to the queen.

"Hello, scraps dear. Hush now and watch—"

But just as he had been at the desert tea party, the feline sighed with sheer boredom at the sight that seemed to freeze in its motion, as if waiting to be fully and attentively watched. The attention instead shown him was clearly more to his liking.

"A wise-ass, a sage, a know-it-all and a crazy man were lying in a humidor," he began. Alice and the queen really had no choice but to listen. " The crazy man says to the sage—*Nice weather we're having here.* The sage nudged the know-it-all and said *I am certain that there would be something in all that* and the wise-ass said *Yes, but I suspect it is Columbian and you wouldn't understand it anyway."*

Alice and the queen said nothing, awaiting a more in-depth punch line but it was clear that they were not going to receive one.

"I am sure I do not follow you, my dear," the queen admitted. To this, the cat huffed not altogether perturbed and flopped down back-to-back on Alice.

"The *know-it-all* never says a word!" he explained. *"Get it now?"* And to this, the cat began to laugh quite madly, holding his sides at it.

"Oh brother," the queen breathed.

It was then that a handsomely feathered peacock (or so Alice assumed it was a peacock, though its plumage was in the fiery colors of cranberry, tangerine and saffron) strutted by. It caught the attentions of all three of them, the Cheshire sitting up before jumping down to block it from going too much farther away from them.

"What a beautiful peacock!" Alice said, hoping not to insult it with such an address. Rather, it splayed out its tail feathers, shaking them a bit for dramatic effect.

"You know, if you pull out a tail feather from one of these," the cat began, "You will find your fortune inscribed upon the quill end."

Alice had to look at the Queen of Spades to confirm this, though the idea of it really didn't seem all that strange for that place! The queen shrugged.

"I cannot say I have ever before seen one, dear," she admitted.

"Go ahead," the cat said to Alice. "Pull one."

Alice had to get up on her elbows to do this, and still not having enough leverage, decided that the curiosity of it must be worth being seen by the Queen of Clubs, who actually seemed quite petrified in at state of non-action and otherwise oblivious to Alice even being there!

"It really reminds me of the Firebird," Alice said. "From a Russian fairytale—"

"Just choose your fortune," the Cheshire said impatiently. At his insistence, she hesitated some. "Oh *now* you decided to take care with touching just anything, do you?"

"My little cat—" the queen began, as though to begin chiding the animal. But Alice was not to be provoked. She sat up fully and took a firm grasp on a single feather and gave it a good hard yank. Aside from the surprised squawking of the bird and its wild flapping of its purposeless wings, it did little else. Alice looked over the brilliant feather that remained in her hands and drew it across her palm to see what it said at the stem. She was most disappointed to learn that it in fact said *nothing*! To this, the Cheshire cat gave a shrug.

"I guess the very fact that you managed the pull without getting your eyes pecked out is your fortune," he divined. Alice agreed to this, her luck not having been the greatest with the strange things she had come into contact with thus far! The peacock firebird took his chance and scooted away, going unnoticed by the two ladies and the cat, Alice, taking a look back at the two immobile queens.

"They do look strange like that," she observed, thinking of the parade of ice sculptures she had seen one winter. They had been utterly amazing and intricate and though the sun had been shining, it had been a wonder that they did not melt under it. Quite of course, she supposed it really had been cold enough for them not to—it had been winter, after all.

"There had been swans and ships and horses and even Big Ben," she recounted to the Queen of Spades and the Cheshire cat. "I can only imagine how many, many hours it had taken, chiseling away at the ice to make such magnificent things as those!"

"That *is* fascinating," the Cheshire cat said dryly.

"Yes, my dear," the Queen of Spades agreed. "It is quite so fascinating. But now if you don't mind, we seem to have gotten very seriously off track!"

It occurred to Alice that they had indeed gotten off track! A war was about to rage before them and their incessant yammering was the cause of its delay! And anyone who knows anything about trying to hold back the force of any great calamity knows that it is usually better *not* to! The Queen of Spades, the Cheshire cat (who was now showing some interest in something that would not directly serve the purpose of appeasing his appetite!) and Alice turned their attentions finally back to the Queens of Clubs and Diamonds, who both now seemed better thawed from their previous state of freeze.

"*I cannot let you get away with this,*" said the Queen of Diamonds. "*This time you've brought too much amiss.*"

"I suppose now *you* would like to play a little game, hmm?" was the Queen of Clubs' accusing assumption.

"*Of games you shall play this day no more—I declare on you no less than War.*"

"Oh you have me so frightened now—" the Q. of C's said quite sarcastically. "Whatever shall I do?" But the idea of a war appealed to her. "Shall it be a battle of wits then? Or of strength?"

"It seems that you've come equipped for one and not the other, so our battle will be a kind of another. It will be a test of temptations, a test of will. Not of strength, nor of skill."

"This should be interesting," the Queen of Spades whispered, amused by the uniqueness of it and a little amazed that not only was the Queen of Diamonds proposing it—for she was most certainly not known as a warring type—but that her nemesis was accepting!

The Queen of Diamonds was to offer the first temptation and this she did easily, producing a very large and overly bejeweled hand mirror with a bright pink ribbon tied to it.

"And what would I want that for?" the Queen of Clubs huffed, but there was a glimmer in her eyes. "I have plenty enough mirrors for the moment."

"But not enough husbands, to this you will attest, and with this simple looking glass you will be able to see the rest. This mirror is not so very common you see—for in its reflection, it shows your husbands to-be."

"How very clever," her majesty of Spades muttered.

And this certainly was tempting to her highness of Clubs. She made to take a step forward but caught herself and remained still. With the tipping up of her nose and a partly hidden clenching of her fist, she firmly stamped her foot, and most successfully she refused. And with a poof of horribly pink smoke, and a flashing look of great forlorning from its once-possible owner, the mirror was gone.

"Fine then," she huffed, and Alice thought that the woman would spit nails if she could—and then she did, fortunately none of them hitting anything of importance. "My turn."

Then from somewhere, the Queen of Clubs brought out a full and beautiful set of bone china—complete with bread and dessert plates, dinner plates, tea cups enough for four, saucers, a tea pot with its sugar bowl and creamer, not to mention a serving dish, a platter *and* a gravy boat—all hand-painted with the most exquisite and non-matching garden of flora and swirls one ever did see! This display made the Queen of Diamonds swallow audibly at its beauty, and even more so when her opposer dropped the entire spread into a large wooden tub, every piece shattering into a million other pieces, and with a lot more huffing and puffing, she picked up the tub and heave-ho'd it onto a mound of sand, where every last bit sank into the grains to be futuristically sought. Her Royalness of Diamonds gasped and she began to rush for the sand, her immediate impulse being to sift through it to find every last lovely bit.

But she stopped, only a few mere inches short of touching the sand.

"*They shall be there later,*" she said decidedly. "*And I can resist. But now I've something that will make your own yearnings persist.*"

With the shake of her hand in the air, she now held in it a scroll with multi-colored tassels at its ends.

"Just what have you got there?" asked her opponent.

"*This little parchment, my dear, is a treaty. Signed by every last one of your sweeties. Letting you accompany through the muck, forests and mire, following suit on all of the expeditions of your desires.*"

The Queen of Clubs' eyes grew wide at this and she took a reach for it.

"Let me see that!" she demanded, but the Queen of Diamonds drew it back quickly.

"*On this you shall have to take my word and know that I speak truly: your conduct does not need to be so unruly.*"

At this, her eyes narrowed into devious slits and Alice nearly shivered on the ground where she still lay, so ferocious did the woman look!

"A treaty you say?" And she pondered on it for a few moments. "It could not be possible—my husbands would never agree to such a thing."

At this, the Queen of Precious Shining Jewels let the Queen of Blunt Objects of Bludgeoning see the treaty a bit more closely. To this, the latter smiled wryly.

"They *appear* to be real signatures, but I shall pass—it is ever so much more fun nagging them about going. What would be the fun of a measly invitation?"

And this scroll too became but a memory.

"Very well," the Mistress of Clubs growled, pulling a seashell from one of her puffed sleeves. She cracked it against a large rock and spit on it before throwing it down on the ground. From within the shell grew a full-sized grand piano made of turquoise abalone. The keys were of white and black pearl and the swirled, inlaid vines and leaves with fleur-de-lis sprouting from them, and wrapping around the legs and across the top were of mother of pearl.

The three watchers could hear the Queen of Diamonds sigh in awe over it, her steps toward it slow and dreamy. The queen of Clubs plinked her fingers down onto the keys, the tone they made causing the swirls in the Paua to ripple like waves across the piano's body. It was nearly more than the Queen of Diamonds could stand—to want such a gorgeous instrument!

But something in her mind that her on-lookers were not privy to, stopped her: it was simply the thought of the piano her own beloved had given her as a wedding gift years ago. It was well worn by now but well loved and it was warm and living, breathing to her as this one could never be—at least, that is, for a very long while. She turned away, the Queen of Clubs turning a raging red and she rushed up behind the flame-haired woman.

"Well then? What have you got, hmm? What have you got to top that, *Red*?"

The silent queen sat against a tree seeming a bit exhausted now (for resistance can be very tiresome!) a tiny vial from who knew where now in her long, elegant fingers. The hot and haughty queen spied it at once and rushed to her.

"*What* is *that*?"

"*This, little potion here is simply two drops, of something that not even time can stop. Rather it is a mixture that pulls time back, and makes age for its taker something they lack.*"

"Speak English," the impatient club maiden demanded.

"*Believe every word of what I say is the truth—this contains the secret found in the fountain of youth—*"

In a word, this was absolutely too much for the Queen of Clubs to resist! Before anymore could be said (most of all a warning!), she snatched it away from the Queen of Diamonds, tore off its tiny cork and swallowed the potion, vial and all!

The result, dearest reader was enough to shock even the woman who had held it only breaths before!

The Queen of Clubs simply vanished into thin air!

For a few moments, no one dared to move. It was the Cheshire who took the first steps, going to where the evil queen had been standing and then pawing at the dirt a bit. There was not a trace of her. Alice and the Queen of Spades followed behind him cautiously, slowly, one queen helping the other to her feet.

"My dear," the Maid of Spades said. "Whatever was in that vial?"

"*What I said was not a lie,*" she began, "*and the taking of the potion did not make her die—*"

"Wherever did she go then?" Alice asked, just as puzzled as the rest.

"*Back to an embryonic state, in an Alpine Black Salamander is her fate. She'll not be born for at least three years, and still it will be a long while before she again appears.*"

"How very clever indeed, my dear!" the Queen of Spades praised. "Why I could not have thought up something better suited for her myself, I don't think!"

And then she turned to the Cheshire cat and said with all the nonchalance that the cat himself was used to displaying at every turn, to say: "Well, my little raggedy dear—are you ready now to take tea?"

And to her he replied with a yowl and they sauntered, tail hooked on lacy arm, away from the scene.

"Your majesty," Alice began, curtsying to the Queen of Diamonds. "Why did you not kill her? She stole your bees—you must have been madder than a hornet over that!" And as the queen took pause in her answer, Alice thought she must have said a thing or two out of turn and quickly made to amend it! "Rather, I would guess that you would have been terribly maddened by it!"

The queen sighed at this.

"*The unfortunate story of it, you see, is that she must come back eventually. No matter what of her is ever writ—that is just the way of it.*"

Alice supposed she could not argue with this. That woman— that harpy of Clubs, no matter how cruel and evil and maleficent her actions, she was a queen of the deck and therefore already immortalized, even if just in a pack of cards.

16. Check Your Mate

The rebirth of the Queen of Clubs, though a little unsettling to Alice, would be a deal already done.

She stood at the Queen of Diamonds' side for a moment longer, the queen waiting for what else Alice had to say for herself, though Alice really did not know what to say for once, though having her tongue taken by the cat was never really a predicament for her, and she really could think of little else to do aside from dig her toe into the dirt.

"*My dear you look as a ghost,*" the queen commented. "*What is it now that troubles you most?*"

"It is only that I am not certain where to go from here," Alice admitted quite without her own consenting to do so! The queen had such a soft sweetness in her sea-reflecting eyes (and now that Alice had actually *seen* the sea, she felt she was authorized to think this!), and she knew the Queen of Diamonds had the answers she needed just then.

"*You must naturally now go where you belong, my dear. Does this, to you, not at all seem clear?*"

"I suppose I must be getting there," Alice agreed. "And though I am most anxious to go, I fear I do not know the way. For really—where have I come *from*? I think I must know that first in order to get to where I am going."

"*Certainly my dearest little one, and going* back *cannot be done. You must go* forward, *to you this I impart. For this, you know you must only follow your heart.*"

This seemed wise and curiously obvious to Alice! Follow her heart—she imagined that she had done quite a bit of that all along, and though it had certainly taken her down some most frightening paths, she knew that it would get her to where she in the end, needed to be.

"I do wish doing just that were but a bit easier," she said, and this did make the Queen of Diamonds smile.

"*You do deserve the answers to come with a bit more ease,*" she agreed, taking out an aquamarine glass vial from her silken skirt pocket and pulling a silver ring from its cap. "*Watch now, my dear, if you please—*"

With a gentle breath, the queen blew through the ring, creating a stream of bubbles that were perfectly shaped like iridescent hearts! They floated on the breeze, Alice at once mesmerized by their simple and magical beauty.

"Oh—" she breathed. "They are so very lovely!"

116

"One of them is your own, you know. It will show you exactly where to go."

"But how will I--?" Alice began to ask, but her question was cut short when one of the bubble hearts turned the brightest, silliest and most dandy of pinks! It was quite clearly Alice's.

She thought she may have uttered something of a *thank you* to the queen, but couldn't be sure, as her feet were carrying her off quickly behind the misshapen sphere. It did seem to go on and on for a very long while—much longer, Alice thought, than she could ever remember a bubble to have lasted without popping. But then, she recounted, this was not just an ordinary bubble—it was her *heart* and she supposed that were it to pop—well, certainly it would *not* be at all good! And for all of the following she seemed to have done throughout her life thus far, she wondered just how exactly she had managed it, when she could scarcely keep up with the transparent little thing now? Really, it was a moot point and she was keeping up quite well, even as she scarcely noticed and very nearly stumbled upon what she thought to be a knee-high pigeon.

"Arrgh!" it growled in a perturbed sort of way.

"Oh!" Alice gasped, taking a few steps backward; most in like to assess the thing. It really was quite ragged—missing one eye, a few toes off of one foot and then Alice noticed—the *entire* second foot! She knew she really ought not to stare, as it was terribly impolite, but she presumed there must be some sort of story here worth listening to! And any besides—her curiosity demanded she stay put!

"I do beg your pardon, uhm—*sir*—" she began, a little unsure as to how to address the appendage-deprived fellow.

"Aye, miss!" it pardoned, with the same gruff tone. "Yar most pardoned."

Alice thought it to have a sea-faring sound to it and it smelled just a bit of it as well. Of course, and not unusually, her curiousness led her words out of her mouth and beyond any sense of manners. (*Manners?*)

"Excuse me, sir, for being so forward, but—"

"Arrgh! You want to know if I'm a pirate!" he guessed.

"Why, well, yes! I do!" she admitted excitedly. The pigeon ruffled his feathers and hobble-strutted around for a moment, the peg-leg terribly peaking her interest in a way such things ought not peak the interests of young and mostly proper girls.

"Aye!" he was continuing. "Sailed the seventy seas and a rancor of rivers—" (Alice was not positive what *rancor* meant exactly, but she was certain it did not mean how the pigeon used it, nor were there seventy seas—and that was a very fact indeed! Still, it all had a nice ring to it and so she let it go to the wayside.)

117

"Were you a fierce pirate?"

"Aye! The fiercest!"

"And did you find much treasure?"

"Aye! The most!"

"And were you the captain of your ship?"

Alice felt it best to bombard it with such inquiries, as it seemed rather to enjoy the interview.

"Not exactly—" it admitted without hesitation, but with a bit of embarrassed irritation and a little irritated embarrassment besides. "But what I'd like most to tell you about, little lass, is one of our greatest discoveries—Arrgh! The Blue Babies—"

"Blue—*Babies*?" Alice said. And within her own head—she really did not think she wanted to hear about blue anything, much less babies!

"Aye! Blue Babies! We had to sail for months, you see, and then travel by land for another several weeks, through the hottest and vastest of deserts, where the Maharaja of pipes and smoking apparati was reigning in his smoky terror—it's where I lost me foot—" It was the briefest interjection. "—But then we reached the swamplands and had to crawl on our bellies like the slimy creatures of the mire until we came out well on the other side—"

"Creatures?" Alice interrupted.

"Aye. Creatures. So there we were—"

"But what kind of creatures?" Alice asked rudely. But really not as rudely as the pigeon practically ignoring her questions, she reasoned. And not that she would ever dare to take up practice in it, but Alice was certain she had heard somewheres of *pigeon kicking* and imagined—despite the size of this one—that she likely could perform it, so she felt it safe to tempt an outrage from this fowl.

"All kinds of creatures. Most especially crocodillos and the like—"

"*Crocodillos?*" and this stirred an image of Georgie and the sandy teatime they'd shared, she could not guess when ago. "Do you not mean *armadile*? Though they are the same I suppose—"

"Arrgh! Certainly not! I do most assuredly mean *crocodillo* in all specificity, and I'll not be changing me mind on it!" And this silenced Alice for just a moment.

"So where was I? Ah yes! We had just reached the other side of the swamps and what did we find there but a whole bushfull of Blue Babies!"

"But wait—" she began, feeling the story cycling along faster than she felt her head could keep up with.

"And though we tried to reach these little Blue Babies, with their puckered, one-eyed star faces, we were to have them to no avail!"

"What would you have done with them, had you picked them?" Alice asked.

"Why we'd have eaten them, of course!"

This took Alice a bit aback, the thought of eating babies—no matter their color, too grotesque for her to fathom, never mind that they all only had a single eye!

"Arrgh, we could have done so much with them," the pigeon was carrying on. "Baked them in a pie, mixed them into muffins, or made a nice little jam or jelly preserve—slathered onto a little shortbread—"

And while the pirate pigeon was off on a far away blue reminiscence, it occurred to Alice that perhaps she'd misunderstood him, and as this was not terribly unlikely of a thing for little Alice to do, we must insist upon its happening!

"Uhm, pirate, err, captain?"

"Aye! I was quite a captain in my day! The best and most fearsome ever there was!"

"I am sure. But did you mean blue *berries?*"

The pigeon stilled for a second, Alice's words taking a moment to register, his one good eye blinking while his little invisible ears and brain consulted and processed with one another.

"Berries you say?"

"Why yes. It is more believable, really—"

And as the words slipped out, Alice wondered if she had yet to over-step her boundaries.

"Why, blast it all!" the pigeon became quite angry of a sudden! "That bloody Connors told us all that they were *babies*, even insisted on it! He'd had diagrams and maps all about it! A documentary, even—" he was lamenting.

Alice feared at once that the pigeon would begin to cry, as devastated as the bird now appeared to be and she did not want the bringing of an invalid pigeon to tears on her conscience!

"Well, perhaps they *were* babies. I mean, after all, you've sailed *seventy* seas, and I've only heard of one-tenth of those, so maybe you're friend told you—*correctly--*?"

"*Friend*—me first mate and confident! The kindest viper one could ever have had the pleasure of knowing! So he had a few slip ups with the biting thing, but who could complain, really, he was so very kind."

"I would, think to believe so—" she said, if only to fill in the gap in the conversation, because really—what else was she going to say? She really was not in the habit of saying the right thing at just the appropriate moment, so why should now be any sort of monumental exception? Not to mention the very absurdity of a *kind* viper! Still, it seemed the pigeon liked most when her focus was on it, so Alice thought it best of the situation to oblige.

"So, captain—" she began.

"Aye—"

"How ever did you lose your one foot? Was it during a great battle of some kind? A victorious fight that earned you fame and fortune perhaps?"

"Arrgh—had me leg chewed off by a pack of camels!"

And this image, dearest reader, was not meant for any kind of serious visualization or steady pondering, and as surely it cannot top the horror of the frivolous consumption of Blue Babies, it is certain to be most damaging to one's mind! But for the record—the pack of camels mentioned could be imagined in two ways: it will be left up to you whichever one will be chosen and dwelled upon as the least horrific!

"Well, that is—" Alice hesitated. "—certainly *awful.*"

"Arrgh! You can bet your bloomers it is!"

It was then that Alice noticed her heart-shaped bubble as it still hovered nearby in patient and steadily pulsing wait.

"Well, I am afraid I probably must be on my way now," she said, wondering if the conversation could get any more disturbing. Truthfully, she'd had quite enough of it and wanted to be going.

The pigeon looked a little hurt that he was about to lose his audience (it had been a long while since anyone had shown such enthusiasm to hear his grandiose adventures). But his disappointment was to be short-lived.

"Well, good afternoon—or—morning, to you then," Alice was saying—unsure as to which it really was—as a rustling in the brush stirred up near by. Their attentions were drawn to a very small girl with such pale skin so contrasting with very dark hair that she appeared to be made of bone china. And with her clothing so drab next to the deliriousness of colors in that place, she seemed to exist completely of black and white. Except, Alice noticed in awe, for her piercing blue eyes.

The girl spied Alice at once, and made way toward her, kicking a bramble that had taken hold, from her foot. She did not smile but did not appear contrary or unfriendly, and she firstly went to the pigeon and put a pale hand on its shoulder (or where a shoulder might be, did it indeed have one). She whispered something to it and the words—whatever they were—seemed to pacify it.

The pigeon hobbled on along its way and the china doll girl came to Alice. She extended her hand and smiled, the warmth from the girl's lips traveling to the hand that looked cold and unapproachable. Instead, it was quite warm and familiar to Alice and that stunned her, words hard to capture and speak just then.

"I know you—" Alice began. This made the china doll smile more, her crystal blue eyes misting up a bit.

"I'm *Patience*," she said. "But you'll know me by another name."

"What other name?"

"That's funny," Patience giggled, still holding Alice's hand.

"What do you mean?"

121

Patience narrowed her eyes playfully and let go of Alice's hand, noticing Alice's floating heart bubble. A very youthful and sweet excitement shone on her face at it.

"Oh!" she breathed. "Is that your--?"

But she didn't finish and Alice nodded.

"It is."

"It's beautiful," Patience said. "Just look at it—" And she got closer, Alice following slowly. "Look at the love inside of it, and all of the cracks—" And there were a few, most them as thin as hairs from Alice's head, but one a little thicker than the rest. "Those *do* go away, you know," Patience stated positively.

Their eyes met and though Alice believed it, she said nothing to indicate such. Somehow she didn't feel she needed to.

"Especially this one—" Pointing to the biggest fracture. "It wasn't nice of *him* to give you that puzzle box, even if he didn't know what it would do and what trouble it would--cause for you."

122

"Whatever do you--?" But Alice stopped, Patience giving her a glance that said Alice knew what she was talking about.

"He never should have deceived you like that," little china doll went on. "Even if he *is* the Man in the Moon."

Indeed! Alice was both puzzled and yet pieces were falling into place all at once! She felt her thoughts swirling into words, into fluttery white clouds in her throat, but Patience said enough and all for her.

"Absolutely, *Jack Frost* and the *Man in the Moon* are one in the same. Why else would it be so terribly cold there? And I know you're thinking that somewhere in your many lessons, the moon was mentioned in a feminine tone, but he is the man *in* the Moon. No one ever said he *was* the Moon.

This was indeed true enough for Alice to agree on!

"He has a lot of troubles, you see?"

"I do now," Alice admitted.

"He moonlights as Jack Frost, if you'll pardon the expression— *it's all his own fault*," she added with a whisper before going on. "He'll always be a little mixed up, but that is the sway of the Moon, and she's a little crazy herself."

Again, Alice was in complete agreement.

"But look—" And Patience's eyes went back to Alice's heart and she smiled brightly again. "There's so much in here—*oh*—and *He's* quite exquisite!"

Alice didn't even need to look. She knew exactly whom the china doll was speaking of. At the thought of him, Alice felt a deep longing in the center of her chest, and the pink of her heart began to swirl a splash of shades.

"I really must be going—" she whispered, not wanting to part from this girl quite yet, but feeling her heart tugging her away. For now.

"Oh, please," Patience began, taking Alice's hand. "Have a spot of tea with me first—"

"Well—" Alice felt herself soften and warm at the idea of it.

And their spots of tea were quite exactly that—the two cups Patience had taken from her pocket were large enough to hold only a drop each of tea. The cup handed to Alice was empty, just as Patience's was. She gave the china doll a questioning look.

"You have to *pretend*."

Of course, Alice thought. *Pretend.* And as she tipped the tiny cup to her lips, Patience whispered—

"Never stop pretending, no matter what."

And then drank down her pretend tea as well.

It tasted like a drop of innocence on Alice's tongue and spread through her entire being—including to her bubble-shaped heart.

"I feel as though I'm growing again," Alice said, seeing Patience shrinking and hopping into Alice's hand as she became smaller and tinier.

"You're the exact size you're supposed to be."

"Will we ever have tea together again, do you suppose?" Alice asked, feeling a little sleep-dreamy-like.

"Many times," the doll promised.

"When?" But Patience only giggled again.

"That *is* funny—"

And she kissed Alice's finger just as everything began to rapidly fade and all became black.

Alice felt she drifted for a very long while, somewhere between life and sleep, and she began to wonder if she was ever going to see anything but blackness ever again.

At longer than long last, tiny sparks of green flashed teasingly at her through the jet. She knew *He* was near her then, her Sandman, and she felt the heart bubble pulsating in her hand for a moment before it pressed in to where it belonged within her.

The light lifted then and she found herself lying on her belly, as her Jack of Diamonds did, head to head with him. They were sifting through the sand with their fingers, the rough and smooth salt and pepper and parsley green crystals glinting in the light.

"It's amazing how big the universe becomes when you're looking at it one tiny grain of sand at a time," Alice said.

The Sandman smiled and kissed her nose before plopping a long, twirly castle turret of a shell in her hand.

"Our home?" she questioned, a vague thread of memory singing through her head, not to ever stop pretending.

"Part of it," he pretended along.

Oddly though, she felt only very little of it was pretending.

"This is *bliss*," he said, affording her another kiss on her sandy fingertips. "Did you not say that once before?"

"Indeed, I believe I did."

The Sandman sighed and cupped her face and Alice took a swim in his molasses eyes.

"Why did all of this take so long, do you suppose, my dearest Alice? Us getting here."

"I think perhaps," she began guiltily, "I was a bit distracted along the way?"

But he gave her a sly and playful, impish grin, which was probably some sort of half concurrence.

It occurred to Alice that she had not really given much thought, even once, about trying to get back *home*, only that she must constantly be moving on.

"Home is where your heart is, sweet Alice," her knave said.

"Then I am home now, for there is certainly a lot of use for our hearts here."

She went back to her sifting, thinking over all that had happened in this strange story, and with a pensive tilt to her fully reattached head, said, "I feel that it has all been a dream, but perhaps I am *not* dreaming. Perhaps this is real life."

"My precious Alice," her Sandman said, taking her hands to still them. "With all of its oddities and nonsense and even its nightmares— life *is* but a dream. And that is the reality of it."

And they are living happily ever after.

(Later found posted to the house of cards' cork door...)

Recall Notice

Four-sided puzzle box
Containing her Royal Majesties

This product has been recalled due to gross
defectiveness and potential harm of epic proportions
that its use could bring to its user or users.
If you have one of these exceedingly flawed devices in
your possession, please deposit it into the closest
chamber pot immediately and you will be contacted for
reimbursement!

Thank you again
for your cooperation and
we apologize for any inconvenience!

A Ticket for Patience

1. Stirring

Patience kicked aside her soft velvet blanket of mossy green then remained, still in the bowl of her teaspoon-shaped bed a moment longer. Her baby-fat belly stuck out ever more from the curving of the spoon and this too made her chin rest on her chest. She was not at all uncomfortable though she lay in this way, even as both of her little feet— half-shod—stuck out off of the rim. Patience wiggled the five bare pudgy toes, knowing she must have kicked the one shoe off some time in the night, though she really did not give thought to the sock—it could be anywhere.

It only took a moment more before Patience decided to slide down onto the floor from her bed, her missing shoe quite suddenly the only thing on her mind. She crawled around for a bit and—giving no such thought to breakfast, a second sock or any other such delay—she stuck her head under the blanket that now half hung from the bed. In doing this, she found herself scrunching in beneath the very bed itself. It felt very close under there and it was quite dark. Still, Patience scooted farther over, knowing that she would either come out from the other side or bump into the wall and hopefully she would find her shoe in the process.

But Patience did not come out on the other side of her little teaspoon bed. Where she found herself next was nowhere even close to the likes of any kind of silverware. For that very matter—no kind of utensil, what so ever.

2. Discovery, The Deaf and Direction

Every direction Patience tried to go seemed too solidly blocked to move beyond and it remained terribly dark. She did not feel frightened by this though—she was too young for that kind of fear, still so newly out of the womb (which had also been quite dark)—but it was simply just too uncomfortably close where she was. With her knees drawn in against her chest, Patience pushed hard above with her feet, relieved and a little surprised when the darkness moved aside to allow in some pale light.

She sat up, the world now looking rather gray and dim and grim, before climbing out of what looked to be her father's piano bench. It did not seem at all odd to her that the bench was not next to the piano in the parlor where it belonged, but rather it sat outside on a very dull-looking lawn of over-grown grass. Thinking nothing of any critters or crawlies that could be under her feet, she began to toddle away from the bench. She really had no idea where she might be headed, her shoe search still all that mattered to her.

Patience's steps equaled six of one and a half of a dozen of the other and were quickly interrupted when she saw a sizable black and white balloon shaped like a moocow floating in the very near distance. She made her way to it, seeing as she got closer that the balloon was tied to a string and to the string was Old Man Pickle.

She went still closer to him and though he seemed not to notice her or anything else, and never mind that little girls shouldn't speak to burly, Tyrolean-wearing strangers with odd floating objects, she thought she ought to acknowledge him in some way—she did have some manners, after all!

"Hey mister, I like your cow," she said truthfully.

The old man said nothing to this, but just then a quail knee-high to Patience and wearing a gray kilt with white rumba pants beneath, sidled up next to her. Patience noticed that the quail had one wing as a quail should, and one long skinny arm—like hers.

"He can't hear yeh girly—he's deaf as a haddock," the quail offered. And then at Old Man Pickle he hollered:

"Harness yehr Kierkengarden, yeh tart old cuke!"

The balloon carrier made no show of having heard the new comer.

"Yeh see there? Fish bone deaf. And stubborn as brine too," he added, pointing to the floating cow. And then in a muttered bit of disgust at the cow: "That's a bloody indirigible fellow, there."

"Why does that make him stubborn?" Patience asked, the whole thing entirely over her head.

"He's stuck in the old ways, yeh see? His cow there yehr so fond of—it's not using the stuff it ought. To give it—yeh know—its *floatiness.*"

"I just think it's cute," Patience said, not having the slightest notion what the quail was speaking of. "What's your name?" she asked him.

"Tim," the quail offered proudly, puffing up his chest and kicking a small stone toward Old Man Pickle's foot. He shrugged when the old man made no reaction.

"A blunderbuss through and through."

It was then that Old Man Pickle moved suddenly, bringing the smell of spice and salt air with him, and he stooped down to Patience and

134

Tim, the cow bopping and bobbing and tugging on its string. It looked nearly about to burst. They were caught under a very hard, partially glassy gray stare and the abrupt raspy, dusty and ancient voice startled them both.

"Why, I used to boil it every night in a pan on the fire!" He tapped an ashy fingernail against his left eye. "Still do too, on Sundays."

And once having said his piece, he stood back up and stared off into space, Tim and Patience quite forgotten.

"Bah!" Tim exclaimed after a moment, before turning away and motioning for Patience to follow. Only then did the man seem to notice and he called after them:

"You're tracking toe jam all over the place!" he accused.

"*Eh, secure the pickle forest, yeh wheezy old gherkin!*" Tim called back, then to Patience said, "Yeh'll never get anywhere with the likes a that one."

135

"I *am* missing my shoe," Patience stated the obvious.

"Of course yeh are!" he agreed. "Or else yeh'd not be walkin on the wee Melbas, now would yeh?"

Patience looked down at her feet as they walked, seeing that she did indeed have little pieces of crisp bread stuck to her sole. She could not be certain but though the Melba toasts were full of holes, they appeared to be sticking with a sort of preserves.

"Ha!" Tim laughed. "Yeh've got *toest* on yer wee piggies! That'll be a good one for the papers!"

"What papers?" she asked, feeling the jam squishing around between her toes.

"The daily papers, a course. Though they're never read."

"Never read?" Then what ever could be the point of them? Patience wondered, though she herself could scarcely read.

"Of course not, silly one. They're black an' white, so they can't be red."

Nothing around them seemed to be red, Patience noted, nor any color really. When Patience questioned the whys of this, Tim gave her a look of bewilderment, but he did not address it.

"Let us see about yer shoe then, yeh?" he said instead.

It did sound like a good idea to Patience and once she had kicked off the last bits of toast points, she was able to follow the little quail in his quick little way.

"Where do yeh suppose it is?" he asked her.

"I don't know. I went to bed with it on and woke up with it off."

"Well if yeh don't know and I don't know," Tim started, "Well then that's a mighty fine relish we're in, love!"

"Well, I guess—" she began, but as she spoke, she noticed a small building sitting by itself in the middle of an open, treeless-for-miles clearing.

"Wait! That's my Uncle Henry's store—!"

She began running to it without another word, little Tim right on her heels.

3. Steeping

I t took them no time at all to reach the small building.

"*Lose Your Head Shop*, " Tim read. "Are yeh sure yeh want to go in there?" he asked her. The place seemed rather deserted though and not in the least dangerous despite its violently direct name. Patience knew she could lose *herself* in her own head, but losing her head altogether? It didn't seem likely.

"My uncle is in there!" Patience insisted. "Maybe he has my other shoe."

There was somehow no real certainty to that, but the quail followed her inside anyway.

They were immediately greeted by a dense wall of steam coming from within. Patience and Tim sputtered a little, but the vapor had a refreshing mintiness to it and so they continued on through it. It was not at all hard to find Patience's Uncle Henry—his grumbling leading them to the front counter where he was crumbling up some black dried leaves and placing them in small square, white silk bags with his clumsy, bony fingers. He then tied each one off with a piece of white thread from a gray pewter caddy which was shaped like an egg and had two bird's legs and feet sticking out from the bottom to support it. He gave Patience and Tim no notice whatsoever. This did not stop Patience from approaching him, nor did the very fact that he looked a bit disgruntled and not at all receptive to company.

"Uncle Henry—" Patience quipped. "It's me—it's Patience—"

The skinny, raily man looked up at her but not until her second "*it's me*", looking most annoyed.

"I don't think so," were his words, as gruff as his unshaven face. Patience thought his short, buzzed hair to look much more gray than usual, never mind she was certain that she was the *me* she spoke of! She tried again.

"Are you busy, Uncle Henry?"

And though he did appear it, he still said:

"I don't think so!"

"Hey there—" Tim called through the steam from one of the shelves, a large teacup in his hand. "Can I—yeh know—try this on?"

Uncle Henry did not even look at Tim but answered:

"I don't think so—"A bit rudely before making a sloppy knot on a new bag.

It was getting a bit trying, Patience thought to herself, that her uncle didn't seem to be of much help. She supposed she ought to just ask what she'd intended to in the first place.

"Have you seen my shoe?" she questioned flatly.

"I don't think so."

"Well, can I pretend?" Tim was inquiring now, wanting very much to know if the teacup was his size.

"I don't think so," was the answer but Uncle Henry gave a shrug with his words and his bony shoulders and the little quailman held the cup above his head, brushing his lead feather aside, imagining how the cup would suit him.

"Uncle Henry—" Patience persisted, on the verge of impatience. "Do you know where I can look?"

But it came again, even before Patience could imagine her uncle saying anything differently:

"*I—don't—think—so!*"

And just at that moment and before little Patience could react, a very fat panda with many fat and slow children pandas came into the shop. The little bell above the door jingled in repeated annoyance with the opening and almost closing and reopening and etc. closing of it.

Patience's Uncle Henry immediately scooped up all of his tied bundles into a large cracked cup and handed it to the mother panda without a word. In return, the bear gave him a very large bundle of fresh white leaves, made an effortless grunting sound and then left with all of her roly-poly offspring. Uncle Henry spread the new leaves out on the counter and sat on a stool behind it, just staring at the leaves in long, bored silence, as he was waiting for them to turn black like the others for crumpling.

"I think we'd best be off, wee one," Tim whispered to Patience. She was not at all contrary to the idea, this having been a terribly disappointing visit, and she followed him back outside in time to see the panda and her brood waddling away, absently scattering their newly acquired leaves wastefully in their wake. It occurred to Patience and Tim then that a bush just beside the little shop was missing a clump of leaves identical to the ones Patience's Uncle Henry had just accepted. This did not in any sort of way seem right to either of the onlookers, but neither of them wanted to have a tangle with the panda and so they chose to ignore what had happened.

"This way then?" Tim suggested, opposite of the way of the bears. Patience stuck out her bottom lip sullenly and Tim put his wing around her leg.

"Don't fret," the quail said. "We'll just walk for a while and see where we end up. Is yehr foot holding out well?"

"I guess."

The quail man reached for her to pick him up and once she had, he plucked and boinged one of Patience's curly ringlets tenderly. She smiled at him.

"Yeh could just take the other one off and pretend yehr, yeh know—non-shod on the Luny," he suggested.

Though it did feel a little funny to her, having only the one shoe, and the ground *did* feel a little more like gray Swiss cheese underfoot than it probably should have, she thought she really rather would have liked to have them both.

"Keep going then?" Tim asked, sensing this very thought of hers. She nodded to this and so off they continued.

4. Executioner's Trophy

It was not much longer after that, before Tim and Patience noticed that they were being approached by some sort of very large wedding cake. Neither of them found this strange and as it turned out, once it became closer to them, they saw that the cake was in fact some sort of neck-to-head-to-toe queen. They perceived her in just this way simply because her smiling head was *in* her arms. And there was nothing at the top of her neck! She might have been a terrifying sight had she not been so delectably beautiful. Patience was not in the least afraid of her and once the queen was standing before them, she asked quite boldly:

"What kind of queen are you?"

"A hungry one! When's luncheon? Anyone have a timepiece? Oo—or a piece of *anything* scrumptious?" rambled the woman.

To this, Tim bowed to her deeply, hoping she didn't have a taste for his kind, and muttered an appropriate greeting.

"Thank you," she said to him. "Your manners are delicious."

"We're looking for something too," Patience said. "But it's not food."

"Oh? I cannot wonder how anyone would want to be searching for something other than a tasty morsel, but whatever. What is it then that you seek? Perhaps I can help?"

"Her wee shoe," Tim answered. The queen's eyes brightened as though she remembered something wondrous.

"Oh yes!" she exclaimed before removing one of her own shoes. It was also white and quite ornate, the entire thing being covered with small rosebuds and bows and a pair of sparkling white doves. She took a bite of the toe and it crumbled on her lips like sugar and frosted glass.

"Mm-*divinity*!" She held it out to Tim and Patience. "Care for a nibble? It is quite lovely—"

They declined and watched the beautiful woman devour the shoe, heel to toe—though not in that particular order. She did converse with them all the while, asking Patience the details of her lost shoe, for truly she was interested and wanted greatly to help in the search.

"Well, it's like a little white boot," Patience said.

"Kind of like Tim's there?" the queen asked, still crunching messily on her shoe.

Tim put forth his skinny fowl leg to show off his white, laced up, heelless boot.

141

"Sort of," Patience said. "More like this one—" And she held out her own foot.

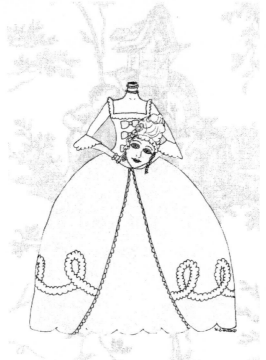

"Oh yes, of course!" the queen said. "How silly of me! Where *is* my head?"

Both the little girl and the bird pointed directly at the woman's powdered-haired, powdered-faced head.

"You two are impressing me well," she praised. "Most people look above my neck when speaking to me, as though my head is still up there. I suppose I could carry it thus—" and she held it with both hands in the air, just above where it used to be. "—But my arms really do get tired this way." And she lowered it again with a giggle.

"It's not so bad, really," Tim said. "Yeh're closer to us in this way."

"I suppose you're right."

Patience was a bit curious as to why the queen's head was as it was in any case, and not knowing if it was polite or not to ask, she felt that her honesty in wanting to know made the asking polite enough.

"Why do you carry it around like that anyway?"

"Well, it was removed and then as an after thought—" She had a little pause, thinking of the right way to phrase her reply. "—a sort of— *executioner's trophy*, you see. Only the one taking it off thought it best that I have it myself, because I couldn't very well go running around without my head—that would just look odd. So perhaps it was more like a consolation prize, or other. Oh *looky*--!" she said, interrupting herself. And they did look off into the distance of her delicate, pointing finger, at yet another approaching figure.

"Grimm! Grimm!" she called out excitedly, jumping up and down. A distinct snapping was heard and it made her pause to kick off her broken-heeled shoe, all the while muttering "Well that was a waste", before going back to her bouncing excitement.

Tim and Patience beheld the arrival of a black-hooded skeletal man who was dressed in tall, shiny black boots and a gray safari get-up. He carried with him a gray headstone-shaped bag with two gossamer wings sticking out of it.

"*Grimm!*" the queen exclaimed one more time, before lifting her head so her lips could kiss where his cheekbone—or at the least—bony cheek must have been.

"Darling," he greeted. "I haven't seen you since the last time!" And he saw Patience and her bird friend standing quietly by. He took a sudden bit of interest in Patience.

"I know you," Patience said cautiously and noticing that he had noticed her. The hooded man stooped down closer to her, his gray eyes smiling with recognition from the darkness within the hood.

"Well yes, naturally. We only just saw one another a few years ago, I think it was."

Patience was not sure about that, being only three years old as it was. She eyed his bag and he saw this. She touched one of the wings gingerly and as she had thought it might be, it was very soft.

"That is my knap-forever-sack," he explained.

"What's in it?" she asked in a whisper.

"I collect stories—" By the way he said *stories*, she was not sure she wanted to know more. "What's your story this time, doll?" he asked.

"Lost shoe," the queen interjected.

"That's all?" Mister Grimm asked, his tone lightening. "Oh, I'm not here for you then. You've got a lot of story to go still. Good luck with finding your shoe though. Of course, if you are still as much of a sweetheart now as you were the last time we met, I'm sure you'll find your way easily enough."

"So how have you been, Grimm?" the queen asked, taking the conversation over and hooking her arm through his. "Been busy?"

"Not terribly as of late."

"Oh? Why is that?"

As they spoke, Tim tugged on Patience's dress and she picked him up again, holding him under his chin this time, as the rest of his body dangled down. He did not seem to mind this much.

Mister Grimm patted the queen's hand before putting one of his hands on his hips and then surveying the nearly desolate area.

"The Bonnies La Choppe have been filling in more lately. Lots going on there."

"Oh," the queen breathed softly, this a seemingly close topic to her. "Yes, I suppose so."

Tim tipped his head back to see if Patience understood of the Legion being discussed, but she clearly did not. No more was clear to her of them, even as one of these afore mentioned came to the quartet only seconds later with definite intent, sizing them all up one by one with intense black eyes.

This particular Bonnie La Choppe was very cat-like to Patience, though much taller than any of the four of them there, and humorously to her it strode around on its hind legs. It wore half of a black mask on its face, long black gloves and tall black boots, and a gray full apron to its knees. It also wielded a heavy axe, which was splattered with the same dripping white fluid as was on its rubbery coverings.

Bonnie La Choppe went to the queen first but she only smiled and waved at it, not showing any fear at all.

145

"Good day there!" she said. It narrowed its eyes at her, looking from her head to her neck and back again. "Nope. Already severed! Thank you kindly just the same!"

It passed by her and only glanced at Patience and Tim, Mister Grimm's hand on top of Patience's head as thought to mark that it was going to stay on her little neck. Bonnie La Choppe took no notice of Grimm other than to give a fellowship kind of a nod, and then it quickly strode away as quickly as it had arrived.

"That was cutting it rather close, I'd say," said Mister Grimm.

"Oh you have such a wonderful sense of humor!" the queen praised.

"It is the nature of my business," he said. "Reaping day in and day out *has* to be rather humorous, I suppose. Otherwise, no one would ever fall for it." The queen pealed out with laughter.

Bird and baby exchanged another glance, before Patience slowly backed away from the Grimm and the queen. The two were both so busy laughing just then and in the midst of sharing a gloppy bit of ruched ruffle from her dress that they did not see Patience and Tim go. And as far as the little girl and her friend were concerned, that was just fine.

5. Mixtures and Textures

"Yeh did not understand all of that back there, did yeh wee one?" Tim asked, once the two of them were on their own again.

"Probably, no."

"Well, the Bonnies La Choppe are hunters. Kind of. It's best to stay well away from them."

"What are they hunting?" the girl asked.

"They're working for the Specters and the text that they follow says that they're only supposed to go after the Chickenflies. Sometimes, though rarely—they miss-chop."

"Chickenfiles? That sounds silly!"

"Chickenflies are aught but silly, lass. They harm many and care little. There is no reason they do it, but still they do. Best to stay clear from them too."

"What do those look like? Chickens?"

"No."

"Flies?"

"No. But they do have wings. The Bonnies La Choppe punish them for their cruelty by pulling off their wings before—" Tim made a chopping motion with his wing.

"But that would hurt—" The quail nodded as best he could with her hand still cupping his chin. He was quite somber. "*Oh*—Chickenflies are very *bad*," she breathed.

"Aye, my wee doll. They are very bad."

"And Bonnies La Choppe must be bad too. They hurt people."

"Bonnies La Choppe keep us safe, as long as we do not become Chickenflies."

"But I'm a girl and you're a Tim," she argued. "We couldn't ever really ever turn into that? *Could* we?"

"Anyone can become a Chickenfly. Best not to mix with either," he insisted.

"But what if one of them has my shoe?" she said in a worried tone.

"Neither of them have business much with shoes. It's safe and sound, little dearling. And I'm betting not with the likes of either."

"It could be anywhere," Patience stated.

"This is true, indeed. But at least we know that it can only be in *one* place: We just have to find it."

To this Patience assuredly agreed.

"Yeh already seemed to know Mister Grimm," Tim said after a moment.

"Yes. I think I do."

"How is that? I hear that it is rare to meet up with him."

"I don't know really," Patience admitted. "I wasn't scared of him. I think he was a friend of mine once, but I just don't remember where I saw him before."

"He's a good egg," Tim said. "But I do hope it is a long while before yeh see him again."

"He was kind of bony," Patience commented. "Is he dead?" she asked in a whisper, something about him turning the wheels in her mind.

"Think not so much of him as such, but more as *invincible*," Tim suggested. Somehow there was some logic in that.

As much as the vague memory of Mister Grimm had been a pleasant one, a very strange feeling in Patience's belly made her hope for this as well.

6. Toads and Cockney Saints

There was nothing in Tim and Patience's way as they became closer to a little stone bridge. This was aside however, from a very large wolf with matted black and white fur, which was standing on top of a fallen log. As they approached and were even closer, it became very reasonable to believe that the towering wolf's fur was matted indeed, but much due to the fact that there were words painted all over it. Patience of course could not tell what they were, those words, her reading level being pre-elementary, but she knew her *a, b, c*'s well enough to know they were words at all.

Thinking it best not to disturb the wolf, Tim and Patience made to slip past it as unnoticed as possible.

"Where are you going?" it asked them, its forelegs (as it was standing on its hind ones) stretched far out at its sides as though to block them.

"Beg yehr pardon," Tim said in a far politer tone than Patience had yet to hear of him. "But what're yeh doing?"

"Begging *your* pardon—I only speak to anyone two feet tall or taller."

Tim looked at Patience, only a little insulted.

"Give it a go?" he said to her.

"What are you doing?" Patience repeated.

"I'm standing here."

"Oh. Well, can we go by you?" she continued to ask.

"You want to go by me?"

"We need to get over that bridge," Tim piped.

"What was that?" the wolf asked, pretending not to hear Tim.

"We want to cross the bridge," Patience repeated in a voice to be heard.

"Oh. Well. You can't. I can't let you," said the wolf. Patience looked at Tim and then back at the very tall wolf, who did not ever seem to look down, nor did its arm-legs ever seem to tire.

"Are yeh some sort of gatekeeper?" Tim asked. After a moment passed and no answer came, he nudged Patience.

"What he said," she said instead.

"Oh. Yes," the wolf answered. "More like a wall though."

"What are we going to do?" Patience asked Tim. He shrugged.

"I don't suppose we could climb the wall?"

149

The wolf gave a sort of smile, but only succeeded really in baring his large, sharp teeth before he shook his shaggy head.

"Oh, that won't work," Tim concluded.

"Can't we go around?" Patience asked, but as she said this and did just so, the wolf stepped with her, still blocking her intended path. She was getting a bit peeved after a few such dance moves, and though she felt as though she would, Patience resolved that she was not going to cry in front of a stranger, nor would she let out the grand mal tantrum that was brewing inside. Instead, she plucked Tim up from the ground and tucked him under her arm, preparing to turn away.

"Wait. Don't leave," the wolf said and when Patience remained, he then asked: "How old are you anyway?" Patience looked up at the animal and saw then that he was affording her a few small, quick downward glances. He continued.

"56? 22?"

"Three."

"Oh, three. Hm. Well, in that case, I might be able to let you pass and take the bridge, if, say—you had a ticket?"

Patience thought her heart had just done a jumping jack, though it only jumped up once and sank a bit at the wolf's last proposal.

"Oh. We don't have any tickets," she said disheartedly. "I don't even have two shoes."

"Oh, well that's no trouble," the Wall informed. "You see—you only have to go and find *The Five* and one of them will give it to you." Of course, he meant the ticket.

"Who are they?" Patience inquired. Tim climbed up onto her shoulder. "What is *The Five?*"

"There's no such thing as *The Five*, lass. Let's go—" Tim said, his own temper rising.

"Oh no!" the wolf began with insistence. "You'll find one of them just over the bend! Over that way—" and he directed them with the pointing of his snout. "He's such a lovely man—he won't give you any trouble. He might even be the one with the ticket."

"They're not real," Tim said. "They're a myth. Yehr ticket is balderdash. "

"No no!" pressed the wolf. "They *are* real! They are *very* real and they are talented and they are *amazing!*"

The wolf seemed so sincere it was very hard for Tim and Patience not to take his word for it. After a moment's thought, Patience said to her companion—

"We can't really go back."

And when Tim turned to look back from where they had come, he had to agree—because there was nothing but nothingness behind them now. There was only one thing to do. Patience said thank you to the wolf and the beast wished them good luck as they began off.

As Tim and Patience concurred to go along the path, as instructed, they quickly began to see a strange lot of things, quite captivatingly, a sign posted next to the path, depicting the image of a seesaw.

"Is there a playground around here?" Patience inquired out loud. For certainly, though she really did not recognize anywhere that they were going, she did not remember a playground being near by. She was very sure however, that she'd seen such a sign before and generally that was what it meant.

"I don't think so—" Tim opined, "Judging solely on the fact that we're in the very belly of the forest. Why do yeh ask?" And Patience pointed to the sign.

"Oh, not *exactly*!" And he grabbed Patience by her hem, suddenly and frantically tugging hard to get her to step off of the path.

"What? What is it?" she asked, side stepping with him and nearly tripping over her own feet.

"A teeter-totter crossing—!"

"A *what*--?" she began to ask, but there suddenly came an enormous thumping sound and it grew as it got closer to them. From around the bend they could see a thick, wide slice of creamy, layered something, even before the scent of spiced rum reached them.

"Are-are we safe?" Patience asked, unable to move her feet, even if the answer had been *No!*

"Just stand very still," Tim instructed. But as the mess of speckled and layered white slab came closer, it appeared to Patience as a rather sarcastically large helping of *tira misu*. In fact, as it rolled—or *somersaulted*—end-over-end right up next to them, she could see that it was exactly that very same dessert. All this not excluding that it was overtaking the path and leaving globs of sweet cream in its wake. Once it had evened up to Patience and Tim, it paused, belched out a loud, low and guttural "*Mockbaw*", before continuing on its end-over-end way.

"*What* do yeh suppose was the point of that?" Tim asked Patience in all seriousness as they continued on, taking care not to step in the cream.

"You are the one who lives around here," she stated, her attention more on what was up ahead than what Tim was saying.

151

Precisely what was up ahead was a short wall—one of stone this time—with a little three-step stairway leading up to it. A small sausage-shaped canine was running up the steps, sniffing the wall, turning around, trotting back down, turning once again and climbing the stairs—*yet again*. Tim and Patience watched the dog do this over and over as they walked past it, not stopping to speak to it.

"*Mad dog*," Tim explained, before they passed completely by it and only the backside of the wall was visible.

"Who are we looking for, exactly?" Patience wondered aloud.

"*The Five*—" Tim began, but they were abruptly intercepted by the wing-flapping arrival of a very large and peg-legged pigeon.

"Captain Seven at yar service!" he offered, all the while fighting to gain his balance.

"Terrible landing, mate," Tim commented, bird-to-bird.

"Aye! T'hasn't been the same since—" he raised and waggled his footless, stumpy leg. "—*The Incident*." He saw Patience then and smiled at her, puffing up his chest and turning around three times in a circle.

"Well then, little doll! We meet again!"

Patience looked at Tim and he shrugged, but Patience could not recall having ever met this sea-fairing fowl before.

"How's yer mother?" he asked.

"My mother?"

"A looker, she was. Though a bit on the befuddled side. I trust she found her way." He looked about and over their heads, for he was a good foot or two taller than both of them, and his eyes became a little dreamy as he began to reminisce.

"I, on the other hand, became lost at sea, and that is when we were attacked by some nasty sea cloves! But then we were able to fight ourselves free and we made it to the end of the sixth sea, where we succeeded in the catching of the Tofu—but that made no never mind, because there was a smattering of toads in robes waitin' fer us at the end of the day! Thought we were goners, my dear viper friend an' I—but they were indeed a kindly sort—had been after the Great Soy Patty themselves—and I was awarded these—" And he showed Patience his shiny cufflinks—one being a knife and the other a fork.

"Who is *we*?" Tim asked.

"Why, yar a quailman and she's a doll baby."

"Not *us-we*! *You-we*."

"Oh, *we*. The Heartkeeper and my own self, of course!"

Tim perked up at the mention of the Heartkeeper.

152

"Can yeh take us to him?" he asked anxiously, reaching up for Patience to lift him into her arms.

"Arrgh! As sure as I can dance a jig on a jib!" And he twirled again three more times.

"Is that a yes?" Patience asked.

"Nay, my fair little urchin. I can't dance a shilling's worth. I don't know where he is."

Tim and Patience could not help the disappointment that began to settle in, but there was no need to despair.

"But I can take you to someone who does!"

7. Door Hindus and Dog Lemons

Patience and Tim followed Captain Seven through the woods, through some black brambles and through a bit of mud, and all the while, he rambled on about this adventure or that escapade. Their ears were decidedly sore from the continuous bending by the time they came to a tall and narrow house that looked something like a stable. Patience and Tim stood outside of it, a bit mesmerized by the turning, flashing light at its zenith. The pigeon was tapping alternately on the door with his beak and then peg leg, until he quite looked like the teeter-tottering tira misu they had seen a bit earlier.

The door swung open then and a very tall, thin man dressed in a white velvet shirt and white velvet pants stepped out, nearly trampling on top of the captain, with two black hoofed feet.

"Patience!" he said, looking down at the pigeon who was again spinning.

"Yes?" Patience said, a little surprised that he knew her name. The man looked at her suddenly, his eyes lighting up and a long thin smile spreading across his narrow face.

"Well!" he exclaimed, stepping over Captain Peg to get closer to Patience, Tim all the while standing frozen, in awe of the cloven man. "I am The Sage," he introduced himself, taking Patience's tiny hand in his to shake it gently. He looked at Tim then, still smiling, and said wisely:

"You're going to freeze that way, if you continue to do that."

Tim closed his beak, as it had been agape and offered his hand to the Sage.

"A true honor," he gushed.

"Definitely," The Sage agreed at meeting the two of them. "I would love for you to come inside," he was saying. "But there's a limit, you see—" and he pointed to the door hinges. Captain Seven seemed to know exactly what this meant, and agreed to meet them at the window.

From then, the Sage stood and invited Patience and Tim into the stable, the appearance outside not in any way foretelling of the inside. The black mahogany of it ended at the door, opening up to a world of polished white wood on the inside. There were sets and series of staircases going every which direction, all of them heading upward over them and to the great beaconed top.

"This way, if you please," he instructed, taking them into a small side room filled with bottles of all shapes and sizes. Some were very plain and smooth, others very intricate or carved or faceted, but all of them were clear and whatever was contained within them was clear as well.

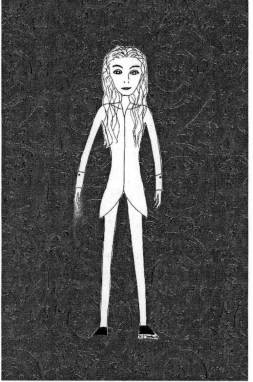

"I was just finishing putting something together when you arrived," the Sage said, stoppering a bottle that was long and lean and elegant and shaped like a shoe. For a very brief moment, Patience wiggled her toes about freely, but remembered why else they were there.

"We are sorry to bother you—" she began.

"Oh?" He could tell by her tone that their quest was of a more serious nature than just their stopping by for idle chatter.

"They've journeyed from far off lands," the captain said from the sash, making Patience dizzy from his continuous turning around and around. "They've bounded mainly across the sixth sea—" The Sage put his hand up to stop the pigeon from going on, seemingly to have heard this story many times before.

"You are always all sixes, Seven," he said. "See to your scurvy, you salty old dog," he added, tossing a lemon to the pigeon, before turning his attention to Tim and Patience again. "What has really happened?"

"We've run into The Wall."

"Ah." The Sage nodded with understanding. "Told you that you could not pass, did he?" The young ones nodded. "Said you needed a ticket of some sort?" More nodding followed. The Sage also nodded, sighed and twisted his mouth in ponderance.

"Arrgh! Do you have a ticket, sir?" Captain Pigeon the Seventh asked.

"No. I don't. But—I do have—" And he shuffled some things around in a drawer in the table he stood at, before pulling out a very small object. "A *compass*."

"Arrgh, that won't help the kiddies, but it is a handsome piece indeed!"

"Oh, but it might," The Sage said, stooping down to Patience's level to show it to her. "Not everything has a price, but some things are priceless, and those usually are worth much more. While this compass may not mean anything to you, you may be able to trade it for something that will mean more. Of course, anything that means *something* means more than *nothing*."

"Like the ticket," Tim solved.

"Eventually, yes."

"And what is the price for it?" Patience asked, this story seemingly familiar, if not vaguely forgotten to her. "I don't really have anything—"

"Ooo-ooo! Let me!" Tim said excitedly, before any fretting could be done about it. "It's on me—!"

The Sage turned a smile on the quail, who was turning his own crossed eyes up at his lead feather. There was no hesitation, no chance for protest before Tim sacrificed the feather by plucking it right out!

Patience smarted at the gesture and rubbed his little forehead, but Tim was all grins as he handed it over to the Sage, who was—saying the least—the one who was now honored. He took the feather as though it were made of the most precious material in all the world and handed the compass over without a sound, save his whispered:

"*Thank you!*"

"What'll ya do now?" asked Captain One Leg of Tim. "Ya lost yer lead—you'll be lost!"

"I've got plenty more feathers, don't I?" He turned and shook his tail at the pigeon, before sticking the compass in the pocket on his kilt.

"Aye, if ya plan on walkin' backwards!"

"Bah! It'll grow back!" Tim insisted. The Sage raised a brow.
"Will it?"
"Maybe."

"No, my feathered friends," The Sage said after thinking it over. "It will come back. We *all* come back. And I am positive that he'll still find his way. In fact, someone who may be able to help you is just over the way. I believe his boat is docking as we speak."

Patience and Tim thanked the Sage for his help and for the compass, though the slender and wise man felt he was far more indebted to Tim and also Patience, for had she not been on a search for her shoe, he might never have met up with them. And that meant far more than anything with a price.

8. Missing Beats and Timely Boats

"**H**e said just this way," Captain Pigeonpeg was saying, as he shuffled just over that way. And only moments later, as they topped a sandier than dirtier hill, the ship they'd hoped to find was just coming in. It took only the appearance of a fit, shirtless man stepping onto the dock from his boat for the Captain What's-His-Name to go fluttering down the hill to him.

Tim remained with Patience, catching her worried frown. This did not last, for they too quickly approached the man and while Tim stood gawking at the presence of the second of *The Five*, Patience saw at once that there was something terribly fascinating about him.

"Welcome back, captain!" the pigeon said, excited to be with one of his own colleagues.

"Thank you," the man said. "Pleased to be back." He saw Patience and, as he was also quite tall, he had to hunch down to be eye to eye with her.

"And who are you, my little dear?"

"Patience. This is Tim. He's my friend."

"Nice to meet yeh," Tim managed to get out.

"I'm the Heartkeeper," he introduced, paying small attention to the fact that the pigeon had winged his peggy way onto the boat and was squawking out orders to an invisible crew. Only the black and gray and white parrot sitting on the wheel was listening and at one point, it spread its wide wings and squawked back "Drumstick for lunch! *Peg-peg*! Drumstick for lunch! Open the galley! *Squawk*!"

Patience's eyes lowered to the man's bare chest, seeing that there was a hole where his heart should be, and instead, a black seahorse was filling the void.

"What is that?" she asked, not knowing really how to inquire about it.

"I've got a broken heart," he explained. Tim broke out of his trance enough to speak.

"Yeh don't have a broken heart, yeh've just got a bad case of *Hippocampus*!"

"How very astute of you to notice, my friend! Are you a doctor?"

Instead of answering, Tim became speechless again, his awe having returned at the Heartkeeper having spoken so directly to him.

"Well, anyway," he continued. "I'm sure I can get it on the mend. I just have to regain my sense of direction. It is so easy to lose your way here sometimes."

"My mum says follow your heart," Patience offered.

"And your mum is very brilliant to say so!" he praised. "Alas—" and when he gestured to it, the seahorse fluttered its little fins and circled around in the chest of the Heartkeeper.

"Would this help?" Tim offered the tiny compass on his open palm and this certainly sparked the Heartkeeper's interest.

"Well, now. That *is* something." He picked it up and looked at it closely and it suddenly did something that it had not done before—it began to flash with a bright white light! He held it just a bit closer, for to him it really was only as big as a dime, but before he could make heads or tails of it, the seahorse stuck out its long proboscis and swallowed up the compass!

They were all quite taken by surprise!

159

"Very sorry about that!" the Heartkeeper apologized. But his eyes widened a bit then and his hand went over where his heart would be.

"Oh yes—wait—I am feeling—something there—"

"A stirring?" Tim asked.

"A definite beating—" He smiled beamingly then and kissed both Patience and Tim in turn on their heads, he was now so very overjoyed. Patience wondered if he would burst, such was his delight.

"Please, let me give you something for it—" He glanced around before settling on handing over the shiny white shark tooth that had been on a cord around his neck.

"Please, take this—" He put it over Patience's head and she held the tooth, turning it over in her fingers. It was a strange sort of thing, the tooth, and she thought it to be a bit over-curved, though the shark denti she'd seen in her time were few.

"Thank you," she said politely.

"The greater thanks are to you and your friend."

The Heartkeeper stood and as he did so, Patience could see that the seahorse was now pulsating with the warm, white glow. It was enlightening, undoubtedly though the Heartkeeper could see that Patience still looked a might bit puzzled.

"What can I help you with, my little one?" he asked, picking her up into the crook of his arm. She told him of the Wall.

"I see," he said with a nod. "I don't have the ticket you need to pass him, but perhaps you could speak with another of my brothers." He carried Patience and a still-stunned Tim onto the shore where they passed by Captain Seven conversing with a thick rope on the pier.

"Ya looked scared, matey," the pigeon said.

"Afrayed, I'm knot," replied the rope.

"Arrgh, aye, of course—Yar Magnus Hitch."

"I am knot," it insisted.

"Oh, my mistake—I see yer Hauser Bend."

"Still knot." The pegged pigeon became quite annoyed as the rope only shrugged.

"Well then, sir, that there is yer problem!"

And immediately to follow, the Heartkeeper, still carrying Tim and Patience came upon a rather feisty crab who was hollering at a school of goldfish! (Who in actuality were more like *silverfish*, but still shaped like goldfish!)

"Cut that out, ya do-gooders!" he snapped, his two big claws snapping as well. The fish only giggled at him, quickly and narrowly escaping the clapping down of his pincers, all the while twittering in their mirth. "Stop it, I tell ya! Ya can't be here, ya have to leave, ya twittering twits!"

They did leave then, giggling still as they swam away, and Patience thought for a single instance that she saw a flashing of orangey-gold in that dismally colored water. The angry crab noticed them then, particularly Tim.

"I'd tell ya to put up yer dukes," the crab said, "But I can see ya've only got one."

Tim sparked up at once.

"Put up yehr own, Patty O'Crabby!"

"Ye're a funny looking quail—" he insulted. "Ya don't even got yer lead feather!"

"Yeh're a fine one to talk—" Tim quipped back. "What kind of crab wears a top hat with a clover coming out of it?"

The crab looked only slightly embarrassed and went on to state truthfully how he'd been out the night before, patrolling while removing his hat and revealing to them the large lump on his head.

"So yeh were jiggered and hit yehr head," Tim concluded.

"Nah. It was more like—" and he mumbled something low in his Irish tone.

"What happened to you?" the Heartkeeper asked, setting Patience down on her feet.

"I got hit in the head with a bison knuckle," he said more loudly and with much exaggerated enunciation. There was a long pause before anyone spoke or blinked, but Tim was for certain the first to do either.

"I'm not sure I want to know," he said, shielding himself with his wing.

"Do you feel like taking a little voyage, my Constable friend?" the Heartkeeper asked the crab. This question seemed to perk the creature's interest. "These two need to get across the channel to my brother. Can you do it?"

Not ever the type to admit being unable to do anything, the crab stood straight, saluted to the Heartkeeper and clacked all six spatted feet together.

"Aye, aye!" And to his passengers—"This way, if ya please!"

"Go on," the Heartkeeper said at their hesitation. "You're in good care." Trusting his word, they followed the crab to the frothy water and joined him at the edge of it.

"Just what are we going to use for a boat?" Tim asked of the cantankerous crustacean.

"This!" he exclaimed, swinging his top hat in one claw.

"We are not, all three going to fit in that!" Tim protested.

"How do ya know? Have ya ever sailed in a top hat? I venture to guess ya haven't!" And the crab swung it directly into the water. Right before their doubting eyes, it nonupled in size!

"There, ya see?" the crab boasted. "It *grows!*"

"Yeh're a mite loony bugger," Tim said to the crab and he snapped one claw a few times in the air. "But yeh're not daft." The other claw joined the first.

"Shall we be going?" The constable's voice was only slightly tinged with offense. He gestured to the hat-boat.

The three of them climbed in carefully, with the Heartkeeper's help, the bit of water that did touch them not at all wet. The interior of the top hat turned out to be quite roomy and comfortable, much to everyone's satisfaction. Patience just thought it felt nice to sit down.

"All settled?" the Heartkeeper asked. They all gave a nod, or a snap or a wave of a wing. The Heartkeeper smiled warmly, patted the two feisty companions on their heads, kissed Patience on top of hers and offered one last wish to her—

"I hope you find your shoe, sweetheart."

Patience had almost forgotten about that for a moment, the finding of *The Five* just so she and Tim could get past the Wall seeming a lot more important at that moment. She said nothing though, the Heartkeeper still smiling at her and giving the hat a gentle push off into the waves. Patience never broke her gaze from the Heartkeeper's light and smiling eyes, the still-beating luminescence in his chest firing them up. She did not look away, even as the Heartkeeper grew smaller and tinier and she could no longer even see his face. Even as she noticed that it was getting dark and all she could see of the shore was the glowing seahorse, the waves continued carrying their little boat along.

9. Day Dawning and Daunting Dismissed

It really was becoming quite dark, until she could no longer even see Tim or the crab and both were right next to her. The darkness, however did not hinder her ears from hearing them bantering back and forth.

"I know for certain ya cannot find a creampuff around here for miles!" the crab was insisting. "That's just *quid pro quo!*"

"And that is just quid pro *nonsense!*" Tim argued. "I suppose yeh're saying they've gone the way of the dodo then?"

"Which way is that?" queried the crab with innocent curiosity.

Tim laughed so boisterously, the hat nearly tipped, but the cranky companion sitting with him and Patience chuckled along.

"Hey—" the crab said to Patience then. "Ya alright, darling?"

"Yes," Tim said, "Yeh've turned quiet."

"I guess I got sleepy or something." She did, unadmittedly, feel a little lost at that moment, though she did not feel at all unsafe.

"Oh, well have yehrself a nap, love," Tim suggested.

"Don't call it a *nap*," Patience said then, not particularly caring for the word. "Call it a *rest.*"

"Very well then—have yehrself a *rest.*"

"Whatever ya're having," the crab said, "Have it quick."

He had stood and turned to look over the brim of the hat, Patience and Tim now joining him to see what he saw. The blackness was just beginning to wane and they could see the shore.

"Sorry love," Tim said. "Looks like we're about there."

It did not matter, for as soon as Patience saw that the light was lifting, she began to perk up. It certainly did seem as though they were on the edge of night and day was slowly dawning.

Quite abruptly (at least to Patience) their hat-boat (crab's hat—their boat) landed on sand. Having been in the water for such a time, the hat had become quite large and none of them could now see over its edge.

"How are we supposed to get out of this?" Tim asked, flapping his wing.

"Just wait, you," the crab instructed, just before a following wave gave them a pushing over, and they all toppled out onto the ground.

There was a sound of heavy metal clanking very nearly by, before a gentle, sleepy voice called to them:

"Oh! Let me help you!"

And the three of them quickly found themselves uprighted on all ten of their feet.

Once they had regained their bearings, they were able to see that they were now in the company of a man in a long gown, wrapped in heavy chains, with a very long sleeping cap on his head. He looked quite drowsy himself.

"Well, what've we here?" he said kindly, coming down to their height, for he was certainly very great in slender height.

"I'm Patience," the little girl introduced.

"The Dreamer," the man returned. "Though I'm quite tired and haven't at all been able to dream for ages."

"Why-ever-not--?" Tim was asking in a voice with the pace of a snail. This Dreamer was in fact the third of *The Five* and Tim knew this. Patience wondered if the Sage had been right in telling Tim that if he continued to greet these members of *The Five* with such a face of astoundedment, would it indeed become that way forever? She told herself that she might have to rub his little face in her hands to unfreeze it like her own mother did when it was blustery cold outside.

"I am not certain why not."

"Are you one of those somnambulists?" Tim now managed to squeak out.

"I'd say no on that. I'm quite awake."

"Hm. Maybe it's yer chains," the crab suggested. The Dreamer turned to the little creature, picked up the large waterlogged hat and wrung it out, before placing it on the crab's lumpy head. The wringing out of it brought it back to just the right size and the crab blinked one eye at the Dreamer in some kind of thanks.

"Hm. Perhaps you're right," The Dreamer said of the links. "They are a bit—" he paused, looking for the right words. "*Labor intensive.*" And then, taking a glance at the water, suggested going a little bit away from it.

"I do love it so, but the sound of the waves makes me ever so much more sleepy and still—I am wide awake."

They followed him into a pretty, though colorless garden, Patience picking Tim up and holding him by his hand as though he were a rag doll. They sat at the center of a zoo's worth of topographic animals, all of them abeyant and enormous, especially to the three newcomers. Patience could make out the shapes of a few of them: a hippopotamus, a kangaroo, and an elephant. The others were not so easy to name, as they seemed to have numerous horns or too many tails, too many heads, or not enough legs. Her attention went back to the Dreamer then, hearing his chains protest loudly as he sat down on the gray grass. They sat as well, Tim on Patience's lap and the crab kind of in the center so he could look at them with one eye and the Dreamer with the other.

"How long have you been awake?" Patience asked the Dreamer.

"About a year." A year seemed like an overly long amount of time to Tim and Patience! "Maybe even two. I've lost track."

"Can't you even take a na-*rest?*" The girl wondered aloud.

"Not even a narest," he said sadly. "It's very good for the soul to dream. I do miss it very much. I've about forgotten what it was like to dream, I think." He perpended for a moment before making a suggestion.

"I know—perhaps if you each tell me of a dream you've had, I may be able to remember a few of my own and that could make me start it up again."

166

This did sound like a bit of fun and even though it was still a tremendous dream come true to have met yet another of the legendary *Five*, Tim livened up to participate.

"Little one, do ya wish to go first?" the crab asked, clicking his little spats about.

"Well," Patience began, "I once dreamed about a really old man with a scruffy face who had a big speckledy cow and it was in the air. It had a lot of nice big black spots on it, and the old man had a pretty marble—"

"That was earlier today, lass," Tim interrupted. Patience paused to think about that for a moment. The memory—or dream—*which was it?* seemed so long ago and hazy to her now, that it was as unclear to her as some of the topo-farm they were surrounded by.

"Hm" was her reply.

She stood up and set Tim down next to the crab and toddled off to further inspect one of the ani-hedges.

"My turn!" Tim said. "So I dreamed there was a dragon wearin some kind of bonnet—" he began excitedly. "And these little booties on its feet—yeh know the kind yeh put on lamb racks, with the frills and so such--?"

"No ya didn't!" the crab argued.

"Of course I did!"

"Ya couldn't have—what kind of dragon wears booties and a bonnet?"

Patience only half heard the bantering as she reached out to the star-shaped leaves and pinched one between her little fingers. It felt warm and waxy and turned to mush in her fingers. She wondered a bit of that soft and tingly gray goo and set to make mush of another one and another, making quite a bit of a mess on her hand. Patience would have done the same to yet another of the leaves had the non-descript shape not suddenly turned its head to look at her picking leaves from its haunch. The Baku—for it was very plain to see that that was what it was, opened its big leafy mouth and blew on her, the force of the hot air knocking her down onto her bottom. It turned its head away then, leaving her to look at the muck-turned-dust on her hands. She brushed it off onto the grass, only a fine bit of it remaining on her skin, before she stood and returned to the dream tellers.

"Yeh've got a better one, have yeh?" the quail asked the crab.

"Of course! I was once dreaming that I was taking a bath in a giant Baked Alaska, before I climbed out to dry myself off in a side car full of mushrooms—"

"Listen to yeh!" Tim interrupted this time. "Baked Alaska! This coming from a Malacostraca who doesn't believe in the present existence of creampuffs!"

"I can prove it!"

The Dreamer and Patience looked at one another over the verbal spat and they both shrugged.

"Prove it, yeh say? My friend, *yeh* are the Baked Alaska!"

"Oh? Can ya top that one then, ya plaid-skirted mimsy?"

"Of course I can! There was the one where my mum was wearin a dress made out of vampire leaves—"

Patience looked back at the Baku-shaped hedge and then back at the Dreamer and he smiled and shook his head at her as if to indicate that she should not fear such a thing there. With the relief of that, she began to toy with the shark tooth on the cord around her neck. She looked at it, noticing in the ever-rising daylight that there was some scrimshaw on it of a spool of thread, a needle case and a crescent moon. Patience did not know how to sew, or even how to thread a needle, but she did know how to match shapes and solve other puzzles of the like. She looked at the placacent Dreamer who was interestedly listening to the recollected visions of the two small creatures, and her eyes became very fixated on the Dreamer's chains. Patience noticed then and for the first time that there was a padlock holding them wrapped about his body. She stood immediately and went to him, sticking the tooth into the lock like a key and turning it. The loud rattling of the chains sliding right off of the Dreamer interrupted the crab and Tim and they all looked at Patience.

"Well then!" the Dreamer said, lifting the lock and looking at the cord hanging out of it. "I suppose you shouldn't pick your teeth, but you can surely pick a lock!"

He tried then to remove the tooth, but it was stuck fast.

"I am so sorry, my dear," he said to Patience. "I cannot seem to remove it."

"It's ok," she said, though a bit sad—well, confused more like—about how they were now ever going to get their needed ticket.

"What's amiss, little one?" he asked and she told him. "Ah. Well, perhaps this could help?" and from beneath the neck of his long gown, he pulled out a small hourglass that was on a cord of its own. He put it in Patience's hand and she looked at the white sand granules closely, as they ran slowly from one orb to the other. She could see, if she watched very closely, that they were actually tiny white sheep!

"I used to watch it, trying to fall asleep," The Dreamer said. "But it didn't much work. Just seemed to make the time pass."

168

"I think it's supposed to be full of sand," Tim stated, both he and the constable crab now looking closely on it.

"Could be why it never really worked for me," the Dreamer agreed but then suddenly he yawned and pulled a fluffy pillow from near by to him. The pillow looked like very large ravioli with ruffled edges. "I don't think I will be needing it now though—" and he followed up with another yawn.

"You've not far to go—" he was trying to say in regards to continuing their quest, his eyes getting heavy. "And you'll probably want to go soon, before—it pulls—you in—too—"

"Yes, good time to go," Tim stated and the three of them hurried away from the garden.

"Do I smell basil--?" the crab asked, before Tim swept him along briskly with his wing.

10. Pins and Needles

They marched along the path beyond the topography garden, the scent of herbs still in their noses. The Irish constable was—decidedly—still along with Patience and Tim, though they didn't seem to mind his company. As they continued on, the gardens and forests—though all still quite black and white and gray—began to give way into a sort of marble stone arena, or colosseum, seemingly open on top.

"Don't know what we'll be finding in here," the crab stated.

"No lion," Tim said understatedly. And still, they headed on into it.

It was surprisingly smaller on the inside, compared to the outside—terribly deceivingly so! In fact, once Patience and Tim and their little crabby friend had crossed over the threshold, they were practically bumping into one another, standing still.

There were baskets upon baskets full of scraps of fabric, laces, cording, ribbons, bobbins, scissors, spools of thread, crochet hooks, measuring tapes, tape measures, bias tape, tissue paper, thimbles, chatelaines and about one bushel of walnuts.

"Hi! Hi! Hello!" a voice hollered out to them suddenly, making them all start with a jump. They took a look around the clutter, seeing no one there. When they said and found nothing, the voice called out to them again:

"Hoo-hoo-hooo-o!"

"I know I bloody heard it," Tim said and Patience nodded and the crab blinked his eyes, which were turning this way and that.

"Course you did!" came the feminine voice again. "Next room!"

They began to search a bit more, finally finding a small door behind the walnuts. It was a rather petite door, though they were all able to walk (or crawl), (or scuttle) through it rather easily. Doing this brought them into a larger room than the first, though still small by the size of the outside of it all, and there was absolutely nothing in this room but a faded and tattered Persian rug and a dress form, whose head seemed to double as a pincushion for very long needles and pins.

The dress form had a face of a young woman, but the form itself was rather worn and water damaged, crooked and rickety. Nevertheless, she saw her three visitors and smiled beamingly.

"Well, hello little cuties! Come closer! Please. I don't bite! I'm not so scary, really, you know!"

And she wasn't scary; at least Patience didn't think so. She just kind of looked like a doll that had been loved a whole lot, or taken on a picnic and then had been left outside by accident and then washed in the rain—this being no wonder at all, her home having no roof. But certainly she was not scary!

"What a pretty dress you're wearing," the dress form praised. "Did your mummy make it for you? You are such a pretty little girl. Come closer—mind your step—!"

Patience smiled shyly, trustingly and took a step closer, stopping at once and nearly crying at the sharp, prickling pain in her shoeless foot. She hopped a little, sitting down then when she could not put her foot down again. Patience was no longer smiling and instead, she set to work pulling the pins and needles out of her sole.

"Oo—I am so sorry my dear!" the dress form said. "I tried to tell you!"

"You ought to be more careful with these," the crab scolded, trying to help pull them out, but his pinchers would not close tightly enough and they kept slipping off.

"Well, I suppose, but I don't have arms—" and she added with a whisper: "It's a little difficult."

"Don't you have friends?" Tim asked her, thinking her to look a bit like a porcupine. "That can help you with your tidying?"

"Well," the dress form sighed. "The thing is—" she paused when Patience stood up, the footful of needles and pins now in her little hand. "Oh! Splendid! Just give them here—" and she opened her mouth wide.

Patience did not comply, wondering if she ought to turn them all the same direction, so the points would not prick the dress form's mouth.

"Come on, sweetie. I'll take them. Just—pop them in—" and she opened her mouth wide again. Patience moved slowly—she really did not want to hurt her, but the dress form seemed insistent.

"I don't think I can reach—"

"Let me help, lass," Tim said, for he was quite intrigued by someone who dared such a dangerous feat. Patience picked him up, gave him the thin, sharp metals and held him up high above her head. The dress form smiled and opened her mouth, letting Tim set them on her tongue. With the quick tipping back of her head, the dress form swallowed them all up! This was a little shocking—if not impressive—but before anyone could speak or protest or give a hearty huzzah, ever last pin and needle came tinkling down through her hollow, rusted innards and

171

landed back in the rug at their feet, poking out like a quiver of shot arrows.

"Oh pooh!" she said, and then—"One more time?"

Patience and Tim gathered them once again (though thankfully not with anyone's feet) and this time darted them into the waiting mouth.

"Well that should do it!" she exclaimed, before once more, the long, thin accoutrements clinkled to the floor. "Ahhhg!" she growled with brief disgust and the rolling of her eyes.

"Again?" Patience asked, circling around the dress form.

"No," she sighed. "I guess I'll wait a while."

Patience noticed as she rounded the mannequin that her back sections were covered in black and white fish scales. Patience rounded back to her front.

"Why do you have scales?" she asked quite plainly.

"Oh," the form began. "Well, I used to be a mermaid, and I— oh! You asked before if I had any friends!" she said, the topic of their conversation taking quite a turn. "Yes! I do! I have a very good friend, in fact. He lives very nearly by, actually. Say, what are you going to do with that egg timer, anyway?"

Patience lifted the little object and turned it back and forth, watching the tiny lambies tumbling and rolling over one another. A few of them bunched up in the tiniest bit between the orbs and she gave it a little shake to knock them loose. She then shrugged at the question.

"It's absolutely fascinating!" continued the seamstressing assistant. "Really. What do you think you'll do with it? Make some eggs? I don't really like eggs. Or toast for that matter. Perhaps if I could get some jam. Did you know there isn't any jam—anywhere? Well, so I've been told. I suggested making something with the walnuts out there. They're perfectly fine, being black walnuts and all—although that would be more like butter than jam. Is that better? Being butter?"

The incessant rambling exhausted the visitors and Tim and Patience had to sit down on the carpet to catch their breath, though not a word had left their mouths during the entire spouting of her ramblement.

"My friend," she continued, "Is such a card!" And here she peeled out with a giggle. "You should see the silly tricks he can do—" Off she went on another tangent about this or that; of snapping turtle shoes and coat tails, sneezing out cobwebs from the spiders that had crawled into slumbering victims' mouths and of letters that began with such sentiments as:

"'Dear cheese and crackers, whining is not a hobby—' truly, did you ever hear of such a silly thing in all your life?"

Truly, the trio agreed with silence—they had not.

"No. Neither have I," she concurred. "Which is why, precisely, you should meet him!"

"I don't know if—" Patience began to say, but the shapely porcupine was insistent.

"Oh! He is very, very near here! He would simply love a visit from you!"

"Well—" Tim began, and he too was stopped by her words.

"Fantastic! Go around my house and you'll find him on the other side! Go! Go quick, quick! Like little quails, babies and crabs!"

If the mannequin had had arms and hands she would have surely shooed the three of them back out into the room of clutter with them.

"Oh!" she exclaimed. "I almost forgot!" And they peeked their heads back in through the small porthole.

"Do you think you could take him some of the walnuts? Would you mind? I'm sure they would be a wonderful surprise—"

173

Patience, Tim and the crab agreed, Patience and Tim making a sort of pocket of their dress and kilt to fill, and the crab filling his hat. Walnuts, unlike water, did not make it grow, so only two would fit without falling out.

"If words were inches," the crab muttered, seemingly just to Tim and Patience, "That one in there would reach the heavens!"

To this jib, the dress form giggled again, having heard him and surprisingly, she was not insulted. Nevertheless, Tim commented back.

"And if feet were words, my hard-shelled snapper, you'd have a mouthful!"

11. Kings and Bakers

The triangular group said their quick good-byes to the dress form and returned back outside, where the sun was shining down its white rays and warming everything below it. They had no clue or inkling of how far they should walk, or to where, exactly—but they all agreed unofficially that the walnuts were making a lovely rattling sound as they walked. It was quite soon to follow that they saw a tall and white, cylindrical structure sticking up out of the black-wooded forest.

"Must be around here somewhere," Tim said, mostly to himself. This was indeed most true, and confirmed even, when they stepped up to a man who was dressed in a very lively (though for it being in none but black and white and gray) get-up, whilst bent over a bed of snapdragon flowers. He wore very large, puffy, melon-shaped bloomers, long pointy poulaines and a multi-pointed hat that jingled with star-shaped bells every time he moved. He paid their arrival no mind, his hands as fixated on his waist as his eyes were on the flowers. The newly arrived said nothing, but watched the man reach out to one of the white snapdragons, pinch its cheeks and in this, making its jaws open wide. The man stuck his face closer to it in a quick move as though to get a closer look down its throat, but was met with a sudden plume of black soot.

"*Tussy mussy*," he said.

He blew up as though to blow it from his very nose and cheeks where it had landed, and with a little cough, straightened up, jingling all the way. He turned to Patience and Tim and crabface, smiling vastly at them as though he'd been expecting them.

He whipped his hat from his head, revealing a mess of a million little braids, clutching the hat to his chest as he bowed and jingled more, and then took every one of their hands—or claws—and kissed them all in turn. Patience laughed at how silly he was, the crab only stood there blinking his strange little eyes and Tim of course, stood there, again agawk, for this was the fourth of *The Five*.

"I am The Jester," said the funny man. "At the service of your humerus. Or your funny bone, or whatever is tickling you lately and *what* is wrong with your turkey?" he asked suddenly of Tim.

"He's not a turkey," Patience said knowledgably. "He's a quail and I think he likes you."

"Hm." The Jester gave a proseborating look and alternately raised his eyebrows while bending over to inspect Tim as he had the

175

snapdragons. After a few moments, he gave Tim's jaw a gentle squeeze and his birdie beak opened, revealing his gray tongue.

"Oh, no. That's all wrong," the Jester said, letting go and patting Tim on the head. He stood up and took a deep breath, adding optimistically, "But that's all right."

He noticed then that there were walnuts held in their garments.

"You brought me walnuts!" he exclaimed excitedly. "I *love* walnuts!"

"The pin maid lass sent them along with us," crabby said.

"Really?" the Jester beamed. "Oh! I love when Pinny does that! She's just great, isn't she? *I love her*! She always has me in stitches!" And he belted out a laugh. "I always tell her it's alright to be a clown, but don't be *Koi*!" And he laughed all the more, falling himself down on to his poofy backside and bouncing as he hit the ground.

"Hand a nut over, would you?" and Patience obliged, thinking this silly man to be the nut. "You know what these are good for?" he asked. Without waiting for an answer, he knocked one against his forehead, cracking open its shell and said, "Head troubles. You know why they say that?" Again, he provided the immediate answer: "Because if you bang your head on the wall—then you must be nuts. Get it? *Wall-*nut. *Head trouble!*" And he popped the black meat of it into his mouth and chewed it up with gusto and a grin.

"Um—" Patience began, but the diagnostic definition was hard to follow up. Instead, she looked up at the enormous white house that was shaped and looked very much like a silo as it cylindricated up to the sky.

"Your house is very tall," Patience commented.

"Thank you."

"And kind of—*shiny*—" And indeed, it did kind of glow with the daylight.

"Well, you know what they say—*people who live in isinglass houses shouldn't throw spoons*. And this *blanc-mange* **is** simply and otherwise known as *my white house*."

This anecdote gained him next to no reaction but for his own chuckle and he noticed Tim still standing chilled in his formerly reactive stance.

"Say, your little friend there is looking a tad frozen. Well, nothing like a little amphibious humor to warm a frozen face, right?"

And he cracked open another walnut, proceeding to eat it before continuing.

"So, I knew a princess once, right? Whose father's father's oldest son would put bullfrogs on a plank of wood—" And he made the image of a flat board with one hand, balling up his other fist to represent the frog. "—And he would tip up the plank—the *amphibiman*, on the lower slant, and he would then roll little bb's—you'd know those as *ball bearings*—down the ramp. And when the ball would head little toady's way, the thing would whip out its tongue and catch the bb—just like it was catching a bug—!" He paused and leaned forward a little to look inspectfully at Tim.

"Say, you really *aren't* a turkey, are you? You don't have that little—" He wiggled his finger down between his eyes.

"It's going to grow back," Patience explained. The Jester grimaced a little disgustedly.

"Ew. Why? You're a handsome enough fellow! Take it from me—don't ever over-do!"

Tim gave a numb nod, taking the fashion tip at great value.

"So where was I? Oh! So after the bb feast, the oldest son to the father of the father—who was a king, by the way—of this girl, would get a really large magnetized horseshoe and drag the bullfrog around by its—but maybe I shouldn't tell you this story. The wording of the familial structure might be boring you—"

Not boring to any of them! they thought to themselves as their heads all shook.

"Well, I hope not," the Jester said when they did not beg him to stop telling the story. "It's been three Septembers since I was able to tell that tale to anyone new. You doing alright now, little fellow?" he asked Tim, though he still couldn't speak. Still the little quail held out another walnut to the Jester in response.

"Most gracious acceptance." Tim only nodded excitedly. "Hm. Still no words?" He opened Tim's beak again and peered into his mouth. "Oh. Well it's no wonder—you've got *cat's pajamas*!"

Patience and the crab scurried close so they could also take a peek into the beak, and there they saw several tiny white cats dressed in black polka-dotted pj's jumping around and doing the polka on Tim's tongue.

"Oo," The Jester said, sitting back. "I *hate* it when that happens to me. You have to hang upside down and recite the weather report to loosen things up. Those hairballs are murder. Say, speaking of that—" and he leaned in a little closer to the three of them and lowered his voice. "There was some news of the Legions being out and about again. But they are really on the move—there was an *outbreak*."

"Outbreak?" Patience said.

"Outbreak—"

Tim thawed a bit more, obediently trying to stand on his noggin, and the crab opened and closed his claws in tense contemplation.

"Of the—" Tim managed out, stopping part way through his sentence.

"Mm. They're looking for anyone with the—*you know*—now, and it seems they may have found the source—"

The Jester was himself interrupted, when a pig-nosed bat with lace wings came flitting down from the window at the top of the silo-house.

"Nononononononon!" it was squeaking out as it sporadically and chaotically circled and curly-q'd around them. The Jester whipped off his hat again and lightly fanned the area above his head, which now was covered with thick woolen strands of black and white and gray yarn.

"Skippy! *Please*, son—" The Jester was saying to his friend.

"Scary scary scary!" the bat went on. The Jester put his hat back on—yet again—so the bat would not get tangled in the yarn, and he caught the bat with one swipe in the air. The circumventing little dear still flapped its delicate Battenburg wings, only not so much, shuddering with a bit of fear.

"Hm," the Jester *hmm'd*. "It seems that Skippy's a little afraid of that subject so we'll just—you know—*skip*, it."

"Thank you thank you thank you—" said the bat. The Jester let go of him and he took a spastic flight back to where he had come from.

"Hating to be a bother there, sir," the crab was saying then in a most opportunistic way. "But my friend here and I have a little score going on about creampuffs."

"Oh yes?" The funny joker's interest lit up.

"Seeing as ya're a bit of an expert on things of *dessertion*."

"That I am. So let me at it," the Jester accepted. "I'll stick it in the ol' *Bain Marie* and have a go."

Tim looked sidelong at the crab, but let him ask anyway.

"Do ya believe in the existence of creampuffs?"

"Oh—" the Jester looked a little perplexed, but took to pacing, his hands back on his hips as he thought it over. It was a few very long moments, with several pauses in between, before he finally stopped and said profoundly:

"You are only born with so much madness."

"I knew it!" Tim exclaimed, jumping up and down and back and forth across Patience's lap. He did not come to a stop until he had bonked his head on her little egg timer. He was quite stunned, but Patience caught him before he could tumble off of her and hit his head on anything else.

"Say, that's a *very* attractive piece you have there," the Jester said of the hourglass.

"Your friend the sleepy man gave it to me."

"Oh? Finally got all slumbery-like, did he?" he asked, taking a closer look at it. "I wonder why—"

"His chains are gone," Patience explained. When the Jester looked up at her and raised his eyebrows, she continued. "I unlocked his chains and he took them off and he got tired."

"Really? That must have been oppressive. But impressive! What did you use to unlock it?" Asked with much deepened interest.

"A tooth. But not my tooth—I still have them, you see?" and she gave him a wide grin to show off the little milk teeth.

"Oh, yes I see that! *Very* nice!"

"It was a different kind of tooth—a special one. And I got that from the nice man with the thing in his heart—"

"The Heartkeeper?"

"Uh, huh. Because we gave him the thing so he wouldn't get lost, from the man with horse legs—"

"You must mean my good friend the Sage."

"Yes! Because Tim gave him his feather." And then Patience took a breath.

"So you've been doing all of this trading today," the Jester concluded.

"Today, yesterday—" the constable crab pipped.

"Well now, it appears that the shoe has turned." He paused. "So then, I'll bet you must be looking for something else. I might have just the thing!"

He took off his hat for the third time, his long curly tresses replacing the last do. He dug around inside of it, pulling out a gray cork coaster, before tossing it aside. It was followed by a smaller lantern, a cookie cutter, a baby doll, a black and white striped shirt, a thermos, an alarm clock set at seven minutes to three, a lorgnette, a muffin tin, an octant, a sextant and a bar of chocolate.

"Oh! *Here* it is!"

The object he had been searching for was very small. It fit completely in his closed fist, and when he uncurled his fingers, this little shiny thing sat glinting on his open palm.

"What is it?" Tim asked and the crab scooted a bit closer to see as well.

"This, my tiny friends, is a pyx."

"What does it do?" Patience asked.

"It carries things inside its belly. Like a box."

"It's very pretty," Patience said, taking it from him and pressing in its small button clasp. It stayed tightly fastened shut. "But it doesn't open."

"If you are on the search I think you are, you're going to need someone else to open it for you."

Patience handed it to Tim, who also had no luck. The Irishcrab did not try it.

"I can give this to you," The Jester began, "In exchange for your ewe bauble. That is, if you think you might want to give it up."

The ewe bauble was no sacrifice to Patience, as she was not much a cooker of eggs, and the unopenable box was much more intriguing! She handed over the timer and took the pyx.

"Who will open it for me?" She asked.

"He will—" Tim answered. "The fifth of *The Five*."

To this the Jester did very much agree with a nod.

"Is he far?" Patience asked, wondering just how far this whole search was really going to go.

"Oh, we're never far, sweet one." He put his hat back on for the last time. "It's the time that gauges us, not the distance."

"I think ya made that up just now," the crab accused. "Time and distance. It's pure horse feathers."

"That may be," agreed the many-belled man. "But time goes as the horse flies."

Patience looked back and forth between the two, all the while trying to imagine a horse with feathers. (It was quite easy.)

"Yoo-hoo yoo-hoo yoo-hoo--!" They heard called down from the pinnacle of the silo. They could see Skippy up there, flying in his zig-zaggery.

181

"Oh. Looks like its Skippy's feeding time," the Jester said. "Please excuse me and it was so fun to meet you all!"

It was more than Patience's curiosity could bear, not knowing what bats ate for their dinner and she had to ask.

"Spaghetti, mostly," the Jester was happy to reveal. "No sauce, of course. But he insists on the very long noodles, so I have to drape it around the place to keep it from getting tangled up. It's like a web of sarcastic Durham thread in there, you know. Well, have fun, whatever you do!"

And the Jester went inside to tend to his friend.

12. Crooks and Nannies

"That was a strange one, there," Tim commented of the Jester as he and Patience and the crab walked away from the silo. Patience carried the pyx, still trying to get the little latch to release by pressing the button. It was still holding fast. She followed along behind her friends, half listening, as they spoke mostly of the things of their strange, color-deficient world, and of the odd changes they had noticed, but meant little—if nothing—to her. There seemed to be some concern in their tones, but Patience's concerns were only of two things: the button on the pyx and her shoe. Which was still absent from her foot. She really had kind of forgotten about it until just then, so many other odd things happening that proved by far to be much more interesting—or at the least far more distracting.

She began to take interest in their conversation when they began to speak in a less serious tone and of a much less serious nature. In fact, they were speaking quite intensely of the Jester's various and funny hair do's and stranger still was the conversation becoming.

"Ya know when it was all—*yarny*-like?" the crab was saying.

"Yes. What of it?" Tim asked.

"I kind of liked that."

"What? For yehrself?"

"Exactly."

"Oh." The quail's tone did not seem at all supportive.

"Ya didn't like it?"

Tim made a less than polite face.

"What, with all of yehr constable duties and such?"

"Yes?"

"I think it would slow yeh down."

"I suppose ya could be right," he finally though reluctantly agreed. "Though when it came time for Ol' Man Winter, I could fashion myself a knitted galerus of it or something."

"That is ridiculous."

"Oh? And I suppose it is glamorous to drape oneself in the nearest afghan and lay claim to being *The Butter King*? All while boasting about *The Greatest Dishtowel*?"

Tim chose to ignore this comment.

"Or yeh could just—"

But Tim was not about to finish, for it was a monstrous thing that stood before them of a sudden: a stories-high windmill made of weathered wood, with slow turning blades covered in torn black fabric. As they stopped before it, Patience wanted to believe that the structure was red—or perhaps it had once been red, but was now faded to an absolutely indistinguishable shade similar to the common gray. In front of the moving blades was a very round, very barrel-shaped woman in a heavy gray coat, with one very large white button holding it shut. She wore a pill boxy fur hat, and there was an animal (much like a squirrel) sort of hanging down off of the front of it.

"Can't go in, honey," the old lady said to Patience.

"What's in it?" Patience asked, Tim stretching his neck to get a better look at the woman's hat. He started a bit when the seemingly lifeless (or at least unmoving) rodent winked and waved at them, the wearer of the hat completely and entirely unaware.

"A *fedesto*, honey," came the answer.

184

Patience, being as young as she was, resigned to the obvious fact that there were going to be words she would not know the meanings to. It was just a part of growing up and she could accept that. She knew well in her curious way how to handle such a situation.

"What's a *fedesto*?" she asked.

"It's any young kid who runs and falls and breaks their leg, honey."

Patience and Tim exchanged a glance, this answer raising more questions.

"Why would a little kid do that?" Patience asked now.

"Because he has a *dersy*, honey."

"What, pray tell," Tim begin, "is a bleeding *dersy*?"

"He has a knot in his heart, honey. Fix your *penser*, honey," she said to Patience.

"My *penser*? I don't know—" The rotund old woman cut her off.

"*Your PENSER—HONEY*—it's come undone and it's falling off of your head, honey!"

Tim climbed up to Patience's shoulder, standing tall and inspecting her head for anything that might be falling off or coming undone. But for the fluffy, organdy white bow—which was securely fastened around curly locks—there was nothing.

"She's bloody bonkers, that one!" he whispered into Patience's ear. The little girl giggled but hushed at his gentle shushing. To all this, the woman paid no mind; she was busy shuffling back and forth in front of the door to the windmill, as though she were some sort of guard dog.

"What do yeh suppose is in that incredulous thing?" Tim asked. The crab scooted up to the old, pacing woman, her large button flashing at them with the catching of the light from each turn of the windmill's blades. She noticed the authoritative shelled creature at once.

"Don't come any closer, honey," she said.

"We'd be liking to know what's in there," he honestly explained, with a claw snap.

"Oh you can't go in, honey. It's not for you, honey."

This raised a bit of suspicion and the crab, having been trained to act on such an emotion, pressed on with her.

"And why not, isn't it for us, madam?"

"*It's, not, for you, honey!*" she raged suddenly, kicking her feet out one at a time at the crab, always just nearly missing, and looking as though she were taking very odd, duck-like steps.

"Ya will stand down, madam!" the crab insisted then, dodging her stomping feet.

185

"I'll kick you with my wooden shoes, honey!" she threatened.

Tim took a squint at the old lady's feet and then leaned close to Patience's ear again.

"Her shoes don't look wooden. Maybe calf skin or rubber, but definitely not wooden."

Whatever they were, the woman was not taking kindly to the very fact that she was stomping, stomping away and she never seemed to be able to catch the crab under foot.

"Now is a better time!" the crab shouted at Tim and Patience, looking at them with one eye and indicating that the windmill's door was not blocked any longer, and if they wanted to get in, they just might want to consider doing so right exactly then! So Patience held Tim tightly in her arms and ran with him to the door, standing on her tippy toes to lift the latch and pushing hard, she scrambled inside once it opened. She set Tim down and together they shut the door quickly behind them.

Outside, they could still hear a bit of the scuffle going on, but the sounds were quickly lost when a new voice spoke to them.

"Missus Spreckles doesn't like anyone coming in here—"

Patience and Tim whipped around, startled at the young voice, seeing only a little boy in the shadows—and hundreds and hundreds of shoes piled on top of each other in disorderly heaps. Not thinking the little boy any kind of threat, Patience went closer to him, a bit of light coming through between the boards of the walls, and illuminating a path to him.

"Little darling," the quail spoke up, still looking around excitedly at all of the shoes. "Yehrs could be in here! Yehr lost slipper—"

The boy's eyes were suddenly wide and in a panic and he put his hands up as if to stop Patience with them from several feet away.

"My shoe isn't in here," Patience stated quietly.

"What are yeh talking about? There must be a trillion different shoes in here!" Tim said, jumping down to pick up a kleet and then tossing it aside, and then a brogue and then a ballet slipper and then a chopine. But Patience wasn't paying any attention to the shoes or to Tim—she was looking at the little boy and his arms and legs and face, which were all covered with bright red, strawberry-shaped marks. They screamed with the color, where everything else was so colorless and silent and practically unnoticeable to Patience now. She noticed also then that the boy had no feet, but instead had been fitted with heavy iron cobbler shoe forms. It made Patience feel for the first time and as long as she could remember, quite uneasy.

"What about this one--?" Tim was just waving a diving fin at Patience when he too saw the glowing red marks and he backed away so fast, he landed in the closest pile of shoes.

"What happened to you?" Patience asked the boy, and pointing to the spots on his arms and legs asked, "What are those?"

"*What is that smell?*" Tim interrupted and Patience could then smell it too. The boy seemed to shrink back and hide, not wanting to say anything. Tim picked up one shoe and then another, smelling them in turn, but he quickly became a bit light-headed from it and did not do it again. Patience went closer to the boy, despite his protests and Tim's half-propelled warnings not to get so close.

"What are those on your skin?" she asked the boy again. Seeing that there was no getting out of the answering, the boy lowered his head, ashamed.

"They're strawberry birthmarks, and I'm not supposed to have them," he explained woefully. "They're very, very bad."

187

"Oh." Patience's concern was fleeting. "My cousin has one of those on his bum. And my Auntie has one on the back of her neck."

The boy seemed to become ever more pale than before and Tim approached quietly, an ice skate in his hand.

"Are they--?" Meaning only the worst.

"They're at home. Well, my Auntie is. My cousin is at school." But then she focused back on the boy. "How come you're not in school? You're bigger than me. Shouldn't you be at your lessons?"

"I can't go outside. Not ever," he began, sitting on some of the shoes. "I have to stay here and—" And he picked up an object familiar to Patience and Tim: a clear, crystal decanter, shaped like a shoe—the very same one they had seen the Sage filling earlier. He opened the top of it, shaking out just a drop or two that were left onto his tongue, and tossed it onto a mound of other shoes. He sighed and rested his face on his fists.

"It's supposed to make the color fade or *thin* or something. It just seems to make them brighter."

Patience picked up a clog and couldn't even get it near her face, the chemical smell was so strong.

"It smells like poison," she said before dropping it. "I don't think it is going to do anything, but it might make you very sick."

"I *am* very sick. That's what these are." The birthmarks were markedly accused.

"You're not sick. You were borned with those. Weren't you?"

"I don't know."

"Well, how long've yeh had 'em?" Tim asked, inching up more closely, still quite cautious. "I mean, yeh didn't *catch* them from someone else, did yeh?"

"Always had them, I think."

"Oh," Tim sighed with relief. "Yehr not *infected*." He looked at Patience and pointed to the boy. "Not, a Chickenfly." And then he looked back at the boy. "I see they tried to get yeh though—the Bonnies La Choppe."

The boy nodded vehemently in agreement.

"They mistook me for a Chickenfly and they didn't even ask first! Missus Spreckles saved me. She was the one who brought me here and she won't let anyone in. And hey—how did you two get in here anyway?"

"Well—" Tim began, glancing up at Patience for help in the explaining.

"Our friend is outside talking to your Missus Spreckles," Patience said.

188

"Oh."

And just then, they heard an exceptionally loud snap of a claw, the indignant howl of "*OWCH-HONEY!*" and the crunch-like sound of what was the foot of Missus Spreckles colliding with the crab's shell. And then lastly, the decrescending sound of the crab's yelled "***I'll—see— you—la—ter--!*"* The "*ter*" actually having been quite hard to hear because her kick had sent him sailing quite far off through the air. It was mere seconds before Madam Spreckles was pulling, yanking and jerking hard on the windmill's doors.

"Open the door, honey!" she was calling. Her constant yanking was becoming so violent and frantic, the entire windmill was beginning to shake. And it was beginning to shake so hard, the whole thing seemed to be jumping up and down. With the walls shaking up and down, it made huge gaps between the boards, so Patience and Tim could easily see outside. The rattling and shaking grew harder and faster—Patience and Tim feared that it would topple to the ground. They looked at the little boy who was only in half a panic, though this was happening and though it was causing incredible avalanches of shoes to come tumbling down just behind or beside or around him. Patience and Tim wondered, quite frankly, whether or not the windmill was going to follow suit!

They backed farther and farther from the front door, watching the boy pace in circle after circle, never getting but nearly missing being hit by any shoes. And the door still banged, and the windmill still leapt and hopped and jumping-jacked.

It was quite a sudden transition—the jumping, hopping, leaping to a still, very unsettled shivering, humming, buzzing. Patience and Tim truly wondered what was to be next! They were only moments later to find this out, for the day-lightened cracks became instantly gray and a shuttered window just above their heads that they'd not noticed before, opened. A pair of long, thin, pale bare arms and hands reached in and swiftly pulled them out, before setting them on the ground. The turf still quaked underfoot, but they no longer noticed that—they were both instead, far more fascinated by their heroine.

"Are you guessing, as I am, that we should go?" asked the newcomer.

Patience and Tim nodded and the three of them ran as quickly as they could from the windmill. The little girl and the quailman followed the woman in the white flowy, translucent gown, feeling as though they chased a thick, billowy fog, the scent of honey drawing them along with invisible reigns.

13. The Dance of the Manti

When at last they stopped sprinting away, they found themselves at the bottom of a valley, and many thin, leafless trees surrounded them. There were dozens of what were soon to be discovered as hives, though they were shaped like men's heads, hanging from the naked branches. Tim and Patience had mere seconds to take them in, their eyes going to their newest companion who stood grinning before them and this alone distracted them into focus.

The woman in the white gown was lithe and elegant. She had large exotic, almond-shaped eyes and a pleasing look about her. In place of long silken hair, which one might have imagined her to have, there were instead thick masses of clear, hinting-at-iridescence bubbles. A long, carved, ivory pipe was in her hands and the bowl of it was also shaped like a man's head, a miniature to the hives.

"So," she began purposefully. "You have a little secret now, isn't that right?"

"Well," Patience began. "We didn't know he was a secret, really. But he was hiding and, well—But who are you?" she thought smartly to ask, before giving away any more of what they knew.

"I, my loves, am the Queen of the Bees. Though don't mistake me for being the *Queen Bee* or the *Bee Queen*. Those are both something entirely different."

"I see," Tim said, with a still vaguely perplexed look on his little face.

"You *do* see," she said. "I take care of the bees. And *they* take care of their queen. Now I *know* you see."

Obediently, Patience and Tim nodded.

"I make sure that my little dears are fed and exercised and that they are tucked away snug in their beds—Oh—" she interrupted herself softly. "I do believe it is about to get fuzzy around here for a few moments."

The little girl and her friend gave one another a little glance.

"You might want to lay down flat as you can on the ground," she suggested, a rumbling buzz getting much louder.

"Can we watch?" Patience asked.

"Of course, my darling!" and the Queen of the Bees said this with a shining smile. "But lie down just the same."

190

They did just this and in mere seconds, the *humder* storm became a thick and heavy gray cloud above them. The swirling and swarming was dense! Had Patience and Tim still been on their feet, their heads surely would have been in the bumbling middle of it.

"Now, now babies—" the queen said with a very soothing tone. Still, the bees would not be hushed. She did not bat a lash, but instead plucked a bubble from her head as one would pluck a single hair, and then stuffed it into the bowl of the pipe. Tim and Patience watched, amazed that the bubble was so smooshed down without popping! The queen brought the pipe to her lips, gave a long slow puff on it and a neatly chained stream of bubbles flowed out of it. The bees, knowing well what these bubbles were for, swarmed around them, stinger-ward and Tim and Patience sat up on their elbows, to see that each bubble contained a bit of swirling smoke. The popping came suddenly, all across the air above them and the bees lit into the smoke, their roar quickly becoming a very soft and gentle snore.

"Off to your head!" the Queen of the Bees said and they obeyed, each and every bee drifting into their head hives. When they had all gone, she looked at Patience and Tim sweetly, before lying down on her belly in the grass with them.

"They are so good," she praised. "Even if they do get a little excited sometimes." Her attention quickly turned to the ground, which was a mere few inches from her face and she took a peering through the grass.

"Oh—" she said with surprise and interest. Her two companions were turned over onto their tummies as well and they too began to look for what was so becoming.

"Yehr grass here is in need of some attention," Tim said attentively. "I know the presence of—" and he hesitated before loudly whispering "*Yeh know*—" and again out loud "isn't allowed, but the void is serious."

"Are you so sure of that, my friend?" the Queen of the Bees asked, before motioning for them to look more closely where she herself was looking. It was certain enough that there was a bit more than gray grass there. In very fact there was moving grass and it was the softest, the slightest, the loveliest of greens! Patience's eyes felt refreshed at the sight of this singular color and though she knew there were a million things she wanted to say, she did not know them to say them.

"Do you see it, my darlings?" And they did see it! A little circling of something long and skinny and rhythmic. Every so many steps, the little creatures would pause and bow their tilted heads, and bring their tiny forelegs together.

"This is the *Dance of the Manti*."

Patience and Tim both breathed a simultaneous *ohh* at the privilege they were witnessing.

"It is the last of all sacred things," this queen was telling them. And indeed, though Patience was not sure of what *sacred* meant, she was sure that it looked in spelling much like *scared* and it seemed to her, as she'd learned just in simple passing adult conversation, that many people tended to be scared of things that were sacred. She was positive that there were probably many people who were scared of this amazing little dance, though she could scarcely figure why.

"Are they always doing this?" Patience asked after a moment of absorbing the little spectacle.

"Oh yes. Always," said the queen.

"And are they always—" Tim began, but finished with "Do they always look *like that?*"

"Every day and without fail."

"How do they manage it?" Tim was asking. "They are not known? They are not caught or—*destroyed?*"

"That is the magic of it," the queen explained. "They still take care of their own in matters of just-ness. From everything else, they have immunity."

"Is that like being indivisible?" Patience asked.

"Yeh can still see them," Tim said. "Well as I."

"Yes," confirmed the queen. "To both of you."

They looked at the dancing party and Tim and Patience found that they were rather enjoying the pretty little frolic of the insects. They could very well have gone on watching them all day long, had their attentions not been suddenly demanded by the booming voice of someone quite new to the two of them.

14. Ockham's Dry-Cutting Razor

"**M**ah darling queen, how do you, take yoh moning coffee?" quizzed a little black and white pillowy man, whom Patience thought much to look like a cross between a ghost, as was his shape, a cat, as were his pointy ears, and a mattress, as were his ticking stripes.

"Black for me, of course," said the Queen of the Bees with one of her melting smiles. The little mattress ticking man then turned to Tim.

"And you, mah fine and strapping young man—" His voice was overly deep and a little breathy, there was so much chutzpah behind his words. "—Do you take yoh coffee black?"

"Naturally," Tim said. And it was Patience's turn to answer this absurdly vital question.

"And you, mah little darlin baby girl: do you take yoh coffee black?"

Patience felt that the little M.T.M. was getting overly into his questioning, but thought it best to answer as honestly as possible.

"Well, no sir. I don't drink coffee."

The M.T.M. blinked his enormous white saucer-like eyes at her, looking for an alternate question.

"Oh. Well then, mah little dahl: do you da-rink yoh milk white?"

Patience was happy to answer this far easier and far more answerable question for him.

"*Yes I do*!"

"Oh!" the M.T.M. exclaimed. "That *is* a relief!"

Patience looked at her friend and the little bird nodded, verifying that it was good indeed.

"And the next time you have a tall drink of milk, mah little baby child, I want you to remember, the great and hardworking bovines that made that milk for you!" Not so much a demand as a spoken mental note for her. He looked at the bubbly queen and then Tim, giving them their instructions of gratefulness.

"And mah good people: the next time you take a sip of yoh steaming hot java, I want you to remember all of the little Turkey berries that were plucked fresh from their branches for you. It is not always so that things in this world are so black and white."

"For certain, that is the truth," the queen said in agreement.

"Yes, do remember that."

Patience hadn't the slightest idea of what this funny and odd little being was going on about, but she smiled and laughed just the same. He did seem like he knew a lot though, mostly about remembering things and remembering to remember the things that were most of all, important. This seemed a very good idea to her. She thought herself quite fortunate to only be as old—or young, rather—as she was so far. It meant that she did not yet have an overly lot of things to remember just yet, and she hoped that she would perhaps come up with a good way to retain things.

The queen stroked the top of the M.T.M's head softly with her little bubble pipe and let him take a sip out of its bowl.

"Why, that is some fine good bubbly!" he bellowed. "And most above all, mah fine brother and sisters—the next time you see a bubble floating through the air above your wee little heads, I want you to remember, how very happy it makes you!"

195

Patience had to admit that she had quite a fondness for bubbles! She knew she would be certain to remember how happy they made her, each and every time she saw them.

"Well, mah dear, dear little people," M.T.M. began, "I'm afraid I must be going."

"Oh, so soon?" the Queen of the Bees asked, disappointed in his need to depart.

"I'm afraid that mah sweet Pillow Ticking is very unforgiving when she puts her knickers on inside out, so I must be on mah way."

"I see," said the queen with understanding. "Well, do return soon, won't you?"

"Oh I will be doing just that, mah child. And before I go: " He was saying to them all. "The next time you lay yoh bitty sleepy heads down upon yoh pilluhs and yoh mattressaysuh, I want you to remember all the very fine ticking that went into those pilluhs and mattressaysuh for yoh sweet and lasting dreams."

And then the Mattress Ticking Man waddled off through the tall grass, his plump form hidden from them, though they could still see the points of his ears for some time.

"He is such a love," the Queen of the Bees was saying. "He always has such enlightening things to say."

Tim let out a very wide birdy yawn.

"He makes me a little sleepy," he said of their departed guest.

"I just wanted to squeeze him tight," offered Patience.

"You two are so precious," the queen praised then, sitting up. "I would love to keep you all to myself."

"We can't really stay, your Magi," Tim said reluctantly. "Little miss here needs to be getting on as well." He wiggled one of Patience's toes. "Her teeny piggies are probably getting cold."

"Oh, I do not doubt that!" the queen agreed. She gave a quick thought to something that suddenly lit up her lips and eyes with smiles. "I have just the thing for it, my darling! Do stay right here, if you would."

She got up quickly and went to one of the hives. It was a magnificent thing she did just then: Tim and Patience watched as the queen tipped the hive very carefully, and a steady, slow stream of white beeswax ran from the hive's mouth into the bowl of her pipe. Just as she was doing this, she blew a bubble, catching the wax up in it so it was a steamy liquid inside of the orb. The queen returned to them and sat down, handing the pipe to Tim.

"Would you mind?" she asked. He took it obediently and she put on her white, black-speckled foxgloves before taking it back. "Your foot, my darling," she said to Patience. "Don't worry—it won't burn you."

The little girl stuck out her foot and very carefully and slowly, the queen eased it into the bubble. Patience marveled at it, for the bubble did not pop at her touch! Instead, the warm wax swished around her foot, covering it nicely until it had cast over it completely. Once all of the wax had settled and there was not a bead of it left sitting in the bubble, the queen popped it, leaving Patience's encased foot.

"Now give it a moment before you walk on it," the queen instructed, giving it a little blow of breath to cool it. Once the new little shoe had dried completely, Patience was able to stand and walk on it. It was quite an odd sensation, for the wax still felt soft, always forming and reforming around her foot and squishing in between her toes as she stepped.

"That should do until you find your own little shoe, my dear," she said to Patience.

"Thank you very much," said the little girl, before she picked up her little Tim.

"Where will you go now?" queried the queen.

"We've got to crack our pyx, yeh see," Tim started. The queen seemed only too well to know of the little object he spoke of. "We're praying to find someone who knows how to do it."

"Ah yes. The pyx. Well, if it is any help to you, the person you're looking for to open it is just over there—" She pointed into a distance that was quite filled with fog, the whiteness of it so dense, they could not see beyond it.

"Begging yehr pardon but—are yeh sure about that?"

"Oh, I am *quite* sure of it." The elegant lady smiled broadly and brightly. "Just go on through—go on. Do not be afraid of it."

Tim and Patience thanked her for all of her help and for showing them her tiny sacred performance, and then careful not to step on any of the little performers, they headed into the thicket beyond.

15. Tabernacle Yock

The two of them took a few cautious steps into the heavy damp air, taking their time and wondering just how deep the mist went.

"Yeh are going to be positively soaked," Tim lamented to Patience.

"What about you?" she asked, caringly.

"What, me? I'll be fine enough. But this *is* a softy to end all, I'll tell you that—"

Tim stopped talking, the both of them noticing at once the wide and tall black shiny wall that was suddenly there in their path. Patience set Tim down but held onto his little hand so they would not lose each other, and then followed the wall with her other hand until she reached the corner end of it. She could see that there was a second one just a few feet away and it went on into the fog in another direction, but between the two, there seemed to be a pathway of sorts.

"Should we go down this way?" Patience wondered aloud.

"She did say he was over this way, and I don't think she would get us lost," Tim said. "Not that dear queen."

"I wish she would have come along," Patience pouted a bit.

"Oh come now, we'll get through all right."

They took a few more steps and though the dense air was thinning just a bit, the walls were more noticeably higher, and longer and shinier. Still, they continued on further.

"This is looking better," Tim finally said after a moment or two, and certainly it was looking much better: the fog was practically gone and though the ebony walls were continuous and many at that, there seemed to be breaks in them every so often.

"I think we're in some kind of maze," stated the quail.

"Hm." Patience kept on walking, still keeping a tight hold on Tim's hand. They took another turn and another and soon they were very much in the center of it.

"Yes. Definitely. We're in a labyrinth."

"Well, that's not a problem, is it?" Patience couldn't really say she'd ever been in a labyrinth before and so the very idea of being in one was neither here nor there for her.

"I suppose we should have started leaving a trail of something or other, to find our way back—" Tim did not finish what he was saying and there was certainly no need to now. They were at its end and the labyrinth had opened up to a large hillside peppered with an hour's worth of black marble obelisks.

"Well what do yeh make of that?" Tim breathed.

"Those are some tall, pointy trees," Patience said, for they were in a sort of way shaped like trees, only a bit more pyramid-like.

"I wonder if we should try going into one—"

"You could try—" came a voice from behind them.

They both turned with a start, finding a very beautifully handsome man standing at the labyrinth's opening. He was wearing a gray velvet vest and black pants and he was carrying a very large bouquet of black and white scissors. In an instant and as was the usual, Tim was quickly agawk, knowing at once that this was the fifth of *The Five*. This stunning young man was extremely tall—so much taller even than anyone else they had seen thus far—and why shouldn't he be? The vast obelisks were his homes. He was so tall however, that not only did he have to come way down to be closer to them, but he was also able to pick them up and hold them on his hand with absolutely no effort at all.

"You are both quite lovely," he said to them. "I could just eat you up." And being the giant that he was, he *could* have eaten them up. But he didn't. Patience only giggled at him, very much enjoying his pretty smile.

"You are beautiful," she did manage to say. Tim only stuttered beside her on the man's palm.

"I am The Beauty," he introduced. "Or so that is what I have always been called."

"It's true," Tim harmonized.

"Would you like to come inside for a bit?" he invited them. "I need to get these into water."

Patience and her friend consented and the Beauty carried them up the sloping hill, past several of the obelisks, until they reached one at the very center. The Beauty took them inside and set them gently on a very cushy sofa that was black and shaped like a millipede, before he went to a silvery, ornate box on a stand in the corner of the room. He opened it with a large and equally ornate key from his pocket, took out a tall bottle that looked as though it could hold wine in it, and stuck the scissors right into its neck. This did make an unbelievably nice display, once he had set it on a sideboard, and the handles of the scissors began to look very much like flower petals, only still with the holes in them. The Beauty closed and locked the box again and sat down on the floor in front of them, smiling welcomingly.

"So, tell me of your travels," he suggested. "How is it coming along?"

"Yeh're part of *The Five*," Tim was saying in his usual astonishment.

"How astute of you, my friend. But we are people just like you, just like your adorable baby friend—just like everyone else."

"*Oh no!*" Tim disagreed. "Yeh are so much more than that!"

"Well, as you like," the Beauty gave in. "So you have made your way to me at last."

"You knew we were coming?" Patience asked.

"Why of course I did! I've been expecting you for quite a while now. You need a ticket and a shoe, though I must say, I rather like the one you have on," he said to Patience. "It is very nice, you know."

"I know. But I want my own shoe back. And I can't get this open. Can you do it?" She held out the pyx to him thinking that as he was big, he must also be strong. He smiled at the attractive little box.

"I think I can probably manage it."

He took the box from her, which was about the size of a small button in his hand. He turned it around a time or two, gave it a very gentle shake and held it up to his ear, as if to listen to what was inside.

"Is there something in there?" Tim asked.

"Most definitely! And it is for you," he said to Patience. "Shall I go ahead?"

"Yes! Yes! Open! Open!" she exclaimed with all the excitement she could bear.

"All right then." He found the button, which was about the size of a pinhead to him, and he gave it a push. The three of them heard a *click* and the top of the pyx sprang open. There was most assuredly something inside!

The Beauty tipped the contents of the box into his hand, and then showed it to his guests. It was a small piece of paper, folded three times, into a little square.

"What is that?" Patience wondered.

"Is that--?" Tim began.

"You bet it is," the Beauty said. He let Patience take it and she unfolded it very carefully. She then found herself holding a piece of paper with a very odd symbol on it: it was a sock with a three-pointed crown above it.

"My ticket?" she said.

"Your ticket. You seem to have had it all along."

"So now we can go past the Wall?"

"Without question."

Patience leapt forward, embracing her little arms around the Beauty as well as she could manage, as was her excitement over this discovery. He hugged her back, taking care not to crush her. She pulled away to look at it again.

"But—what is the crown for?"

"That is for you to decided, my dear one."

"It *is* yeh," Tim interjected. "Yeh were born—" and he lowered his voice. "—*To the purple*."

"I *am*?" She looked at the ticket and then at the Beauty. "*Am I?*"

"I would say you are."

"What does that mean?" she asked then.

"It means you are a princess," the Beauty explained. And though this was divine information indeed, Patience knew there were other impertinent answers to be had.

"Will we be able to get back to the Wall?" she asked then.

The Beauty gave her another one of his sweet smiles.

"I have faith that you will."

Patience showed the pyx to Tim.

"Do we need this anymore?"

"I don't think so—" He was rather intrigued with the ticket by now, and still very much so with the Beauty, of course.

Patience handed the pyx back to the Beauty.

"Do you want it?" she offered.

"I would be honored to have it. It seems that I have misplaced mine, and so I would welcome its addition. You can never have too many of these for your yock."

She set it into his hand again, the little box flashing in his palm.

"You're a very nice man," she complimented him.

"Why thank you. You are a very sweet little girl."

He looked at Tim, who seemed in a pleasant daze, having completed his introductions to the entirety of *The Five*.

"And you are a fine quailman."

And Tim fell over and fainted. Patience giggled, hiding her face on the Beauty's shoulder. He was chuckling as well, but they were interrupted when there came a rapping on the door.

"Pardon me, my dear. Let me see who that is."

The Beauty arose and went to the door, opening it up and finding that the caller was in fact there for Patience and Tim. He stepped aside, revealing that it was the slightly battered constable crab. Patience was very pleased and relieved to see him, and though he was in a slightly cranky mood, he seemed rather happy to see them as well.

He tipped his hat with his claw, and shuffled into the room at the Beauty's invitation. He noticed Tim at once, still out cold on the floor, and knowing quite well how to handle such a serious medical situation, stuck the clover on his hat right up against Tim's beak. It brought him around quite immediately!

"Who, what, where and why?"

"And how," added the crab, putting his hat back on. "Are ya quite through now, lad? It seems I'm just in time."

"Look! Look!" Patience said, waving the ticket in the crab's shelled face. "We have it now! And look—This is the Beauty."

The Beauty and the crustacean exchanged a nod of pleasantries.

"Good to see you again," the Beauty said. "I'll see you next Tuesday for Ash Wednesday?"

"With bells," he promised.

"Fantastic," the Beauty expressed. He looked at Tim then who was rubbing his forehead, for it pained a little from the coming-to of the clover and it itched a bit otherwise. "Seems your little friend is growing back his feather now."

And truly it *was* growing back! It was a thin, wee, fragile thing, but it was definitely making its way out of the little quail's noggin. This realization quite energized Tim and he bounced up onto his feet, his hand and wing on his hips. He took a very deep breath to fill his little lungs and was ready to be off.

"Well then," the Beauty gave in. "I suppose I should let you all go."

He shook wing and claw with the fellows before he picked Patience up as though she were just a little baby doll. His eyes smiled at her with a sugary meltiness that she felt she could just fall into for a nice long rest; such was the sweet safeness of them.

"You will take care now," he half asked, half stated to her. She nodded. "Keep being a good little girl. We will always keep you safe," he promised.

Patience hugged him tightly around his neck, his dark silky curls tickling her nose and smelling of warm amber. He placed her back on her feet and she went outside to meet up with her friends, the excitement of the ticket returning as she realized it was still in her hands. It was not a moment before they began to walk on.

"So how was yehr flight?" Tim asked the crab.

"Not too bad. I ended up in a bucket of gruel, but the mistress cooking it was to my great fortune, a vegetarian. She scooped me out toot sweet and sent me on my way."

"That *was* most fortunate!"

"I'll say."

"Good to see yeh getting yehr exercise too, by the way. And yeh're blowing off some of that steam."

"Are ya kidding? I've got fire for days!" the crab begged to differ.

16. F.I.R.K.I.N.
(Found In Restaurant, Killer Is Nabbed)

Patience could not take her eyes off of the ticket in her hand. One would think it had been made of gold or some other such precious material by the way she gave it her attention. It was a wonder that she did not run into anything in front of her, though her devoted Tim was keeping a constant hand clenched around the hem of her dress to guide her.

"I am bloody starving," the constable was saying. "Starving for something good!"

"I hear yehr innards rumbling like a barge on a midnight sea," Tim agreed and Patience, though she wasn't hungry at all and quite satisfied with the little ticket, felt she could use a little rest off of her feet.

It was a very short walk for the three of them, before they came upon the crab's most favorite establishment: *The Blabbermouth Firkin.* Patience looked up when this same said place stood before them, wondering how a building could look any more inviting: as it was, *The Blabbermouth Firkin* was shining silver in the light and was shaped like the most glorious calliope that ever there was! From where they were outside, they could hear the music coming from within, and there was no need for them to hesitate further.

There was a great hustle and bustle inside, though they were all rather small and there was no waiting for a table. They were seated immediately and given menus to look over. Patience stuck to looking at her ticket and the crab waved off his option of looking over the list with one claw. Tim was too distracted by the other patrons and the wait staff to take a look at the fare.

Darting back and forth across the room were the waiters, each one appearing to be very thin, though as they were dressed in an exceedingly round uniform of sorts that tapered down to their feet, they looked more like spinning toy tops than anything else. This did catch Patience's eyes in a mesmerizing sort of way, and she gave the ticket absently to Tim to hold in his pocket for safekeeping. He too was watching the darting, twirling, whirling Dervishing waiters, their black and white swirls only appearing when they stopped moving. Otherwise, as expected, they were quite gray.

In moments, their own table was visited by one of these very patient servers. The one who was there to assist them seemed rather content to be standing still with them and not spinning for the moment, though Patience did notice that his eyes were very crossed and it seemed that there was no undoing of that!

"I'll have the stuffed shirts, if ya please," said the crab. "Extra starch and double the butter and the other accoutrements."

"And for you sirs?" the waiter said to Patience and Tim. Patience shrugged at Tim and he waved the waiter away. It was only after he had gone that Patience started to feel a little thirsty for a sarsaparilla, but she didn't have a chance to ask for anything before the man spun away.

It was quite odd that as soon as the waiter had spun away and gone through one of the swinging doors to the kitchen, he was spinning right back out of it with a tray on one hand, whatever was on it, hanging on for its dear life. In a clatter, the waiter set the tray on the table, before spinning off on his way to another customer.

Sitting on the presented white china plate was a row of very fat shrimp. They had their chests rounded out and they were quite frilly, Patience thought.

"Headless jerks!" Tim exclaimed of the shrimps. "They look puffed up with rabies!"

"Just how they are best," the crab said, giving them a nudge to get moving. Just as he did this, they lined up on the plate and began to do some sort of acrobatic feat. Tim cared nothing of it, spying instead the little bowl of chutney next to the plate.

"Oh! *I love it*! May I?"

"Yes, yes," the crab said to quiet him. Patience could not quite figure how to take the performing shrimps, other than the fact that they were particularly funny and she felt like giggling about them. Tim made quickly to shove as much of the chutney up his little striped sleeve as possible. The crab saw him doing this and rolled his eyes around.

"Yeh don't mind, do yeh? I know yeh probably won't like it." And the crab truly did not mind.

This was all to be interrupted and quite quickly, as the three of them suddenly noticed a bit of a fooferaw going on a few tables over. One of the waiters was speaking heatedly to a bowl of Czarnina, who in turn was insisting on ordering a bowl of black pudding.

"I *am* sorry sir, you cannot order a bowl of *yourself*," the waiter was insisting. The Czarnina would have none of this and made a few idle threats, none of which Patience could understand, for the Czarnina was terribly thick and its English was quite poor. The waiter gave up quickly though, twirling away through the swinging doors, and in countless seconds (for they happened so fast), three Bonnies La Choppe burst into the restaurant!

"Uh, oh! Take cover, love!" Tim said to Patience and she and the crab and the quail all dove down under the table.

They were just in time too, for the Bonnies La Choppe asked no questions to the bowl of Czarnina. There was an immediate accusation of guilt—for the pudding was not *black*: it was *brown*—and before anyone could think otherwise, one Bonnie La Choppe raised its axe high overhead and brought it down hard right into the bowl! This of course made a grand mess of everything! There was a terrible explosiveness and thick, brownish splatter everywhere—no surface near the table had been spared. In only moments to follow, the Bonnie La Choppe who had done the chopping was pulling a large crinkled pair of wings from what little was left in the bowl and held them up in the air while everyone in the restaurant—even the little stuffed shirts—just watched. At the gesture, another figure materialized next to the assassins.

This was a frightening and ghostly figure of an emaciated woman, her white hair and thin white clothing floating around her like air; her eyes empty and cataract-white, her lips stitched shut with thick, white 'x's. She made no sound at all and everyone there could see right through her.

"*The Collector Specter*—" Tim breathed, nearly inaudibly.

They continued to watch from beneath the table, as did so many other patrons of the restaurant, as the Specter took the wings from the Bonnie La Choppe and then opened a little box she had in one thin and filmy hand. From inside, she took out a bit of crumbled and powdery herb and sprinkled it down over the heads of the Bonnies La Choppe as some sort of exchange. They raised their noses toward it in the air, snorted and purred and bumped into each other. They did not seem to be at all annoyed by this and instead followed one another back outside, the incident completely over with.

And then the Collector Specter was gone as well, vanishing into the thin air that she had come from.

"What did she give them? Was that a Chickenfly in the bowl? What was that lady? Is the Chickenfly gone now?" Patience was asking all at once, as they crawled out from under the table, and everyone else in the establishment did the same, going back to as they were before the incident.

"She gave them a bit of pixie dust," Tim explained with nonchalance.

"I'm pretty sure that was *Nepeta Cataria,*" the crab disagreed.

"Well, whatever. Yes, it was a Chickenfly, love, and that *lady* thing makes sure that the *evil* thing doesn't ever harm anyone again."

"It's dead, isn't it?" Patience asked bluntly. Tim and the crab hesitated in answering her, but as she seemed not too disturbed by it, or at least seemed to understand the reasoning behind it, they nodded in confirmation.

"Oh. Can I see the ticket again?" she asked then, her attention obviously turned. Tim faithfully obliged and she looked it over, turning it around and over and looking at it from its thinnest sides. It was very thin, just like any other piece of paper or a pound note or a sweets wrapper, but when she looked at it from its thin sides, Patience thought for certain that she could see some writing on it. It was of course very small and so she didn't bother to ask Tim or the crab what it might say.

"Are your shrimps done doing their backwards act?" she asked the crab then, seeing as the shrimps were now just sitting about on the plate, holding and dealing out tiny cards to one another and smoking very tiny cigars. One of them even appeared to have a monocle though Patience could not see its eye—if it did indeed have one.

"Aye, I suppose so," the crab said, turning one eye back and forth as if to graze the room with it.

"It is time we should be getting back to the Wall," Tim said, and though Patience did not notice it, there was a bit of sadness in his words.

"Goody!" she exclaimed instead, picking them both up, one under each arm.

208

17. Wally Gagging

Patience stepped outside with a hop in her little lop-sided steps, and she paused to look around, a little unsure of which direction they should head.

"We have been all over the place," she said. "I don't know where to go now."

Tim climbed up onto her should and then her head, clinging to her bow with his fist and beak to get up there, and he looked about to scout out the area.

"Well there is a path over that way—" and he pointed with his wing to a path that was lined with cockleshells and tall white paper toques that all made a rasty and rustley sound when the breeze blew past them. "And then, there's one over that way—" and he pointed in another direction to a path lined with bushes that had fine white tulle netting for their foliage. "Oh! And one over there. It seems to be a little over-crowded all up and down it, but that shouldn't be a bother. Our pick is a horse apiece, love."

"Well that is some fine navigating, I must say," said the crab with some sarcasm.

"No yeh mustn't," Tim disagreed. "Yeh mustn't say anything at all. Let's go on the middle one," he suggested, which happened to be the one with countless stony statues and epitaph-laden headstones flanking its sides.

Patience went along down that one, still carrying her little friends and she made sure to step carefully, for the path was scattered with some sharp gravel, and none of it was at all of smooth and flat ground. The two bordering cemeteries of sorts were indeed very densely packed into their short, tight-fenced boundaries. It seemed that where one monument's base ended, another began and the towering Seraphim and Cherubim, and Celtic, Trefoil and Maltese crosses and Ogee, Peon, Serpentine and Scotia-cornered Square tops—they all seemed to be endless.

"So," Tim began, inquiring of the crab as they traveled. "Yehr stuffed shirts were pretty good, eh?"

"Not as good as the chewy jellies" he said, before explaining to Patience what *chewy jellies* were. "Those are, of my opinion, *the best* ya can get at the *Blabbermouth*. The waiter brings them to ya on a little tray and each one is sitting inside a little dovecote hole. Ya have to coax them out of their holes by reciting things to them."

"What kinds of things?" Patience asked.

"Shakespearian sonnets, usually. I think three apiece gets them out and there are about nine of the jellies in an order."

"That sounds like a lot of sonnets," Patience said. "Is it a lot to memorize?"

"Not much. And they usually respond quickly—" and here he demonstrated exactly these recitations entirely:

"Shakespearian sonnet one, Shakespearian sonnet two, Shakespearian sonnet three—" and so on up to *Shakespearian sonnet twenty-seven.*

Patience could hear Tim groan.

"And then what?"

"And then they are out!" the crab said, walking on his own as Patience set him down on the ground, for the path was becoming even more narrow and both fences had ended—or disappeared—and the stones were closing in like poorly arranged teeth. Patience had to use both hands and feet to get through or over them now, and occasionally she had to squeeze between them to find more space.

"Then what do they do?" Patience asked the crab of the chewy jellies.

"Oh! Then, *then*—they curl up and you poke at them with a set of tines."

"Jelly rolls, sounds like," Tim said, still atop Patience's head.

"Not at all. That is entirely different!" insisted the constable.

"Doesn't it hurt them when you poke them?" Patience asked innocently enough, knowing that she herself did not care for it much when the adults poked her in her little ribs as a gesture to give her a bit of a tickle.

"They rather enjoy it. The more you poke at them the more tightly they curl up. It is such a joy! I'd say they are my favorite second only to the little Octi-hut, which is a little octopus madam inside a small raffia hut of sticky rice. Sometime they let you trade in the sticky rice for glass noodles, though the little madam doesn't much like it. She dances around on the glass noodles and breaks it under her many little feet. Ya really could fall in love with her. *Much* better than the stuffed shirts that just seem to twirl and whirl around and make a fat spectacle of themselves."

"Well, I thought they were good," Tim said under his breath.

"Well, it wasn't as though they were neurobats or anything. How is your chutney, by the way?" the crab asked, for once coming out of his argumentative mood.

Tim searched in the cuff of his shirtsleeve.

"Ah! It seems to have turned already! How fancy of that! Here love--" he said to Patience.

He then shook a bit of it out into her hand. It looked nothing like the soggy bits of black slices that they had been in the restaurant, but rather they were now more like black and white tiny pastilles mixed in with something that kind of looked like gray birdseed. Patience gave it a little sniff—it smelled very much like anise seed. She tasted a bit and found it to be very much like black licorice. While it was rather pleasant to her palette, the seed became quickly tiresome to chew and it felt very much like she was chewing on sawdust. When the bird and crab weren't particularly looking, she spit them quite out!

It was only a matter of moments after that, before Patience found herself stuck in the middle of a round of headstones and statues, and as a matter of fact, she was quite trapped.

"Uh, oh—" she said.

"Hm," Tim said and the constable tapped one of his hard feet against the granite.

"Now what?" Patience asked, standing as tall as she could on her tippy toes. She still could not see over the tops of the stones. She tried to climb up one of them, but they were all polished like mirrors and there was no getting up one without slipping right back down.

"Alright, hold me up," Tim instructed, and she did so, holding his little booted feet in her hands. He teetered a bit but firmed up quickly, shielding his eyes with his wing.

"*There! Right there!*" he exclaimed.

"There, what's there? Where?" she asked, jumping up and down and jostling him around.

"There is a school of flying fish coming this way. When I tell yeh to, grab on to one of them. Would yeh mind, mate?" he said to the crab. The crab sniffed in response and Patience picked him up as well, holding them both over her head now.

It was a few moments before the sound of very loud whirling and humming like that of an engine came close enough to hear.

"Get ready—" Tim said in preparation. Patience could hear the flying fish now, thinking them to sound like they were purring, and in seconds they were going over-head—quite slowly—bringing with them, a very fishy-smelling warmth.

"Up! Up!" Tim shouted and Patience jumped as high as she could, the crab snapping onto a pair of gills with both claws. Tim took hold as well, catching on to one of the fish's coattails. It was very quickly then that they were hoisted up into the air, and they flew along with the scaled school, over the land below.

Patience did not worry much of the height they were at, for it really wasn't very high at all, and it felt kind of nice to be up there floating and being able to look around. She found it fascinating that the ground was decorated with the shapes of cogwheels. They were impressions in the ground itself, and contrasted blacks and grays and whites as though painted on the dirt. There were fields where the pale grass was cut short so the clockwork shapes would stand out. Even the shorter trees were arranged in this working order. Patience thought for a moment as she drifted that she could see the gears moving to make one another turn. She thought for this moment that she could hear the tick-tock of a clock, but realized that it was the low droning of the fish wings flapping through the air. She looked up at them, their amassed silver bodies flashing and shining in the light like the underbelly of a zeppelin. It really was quite magnificent.

It was then that something else caught her eye. In truth, it was something that caught her ear: a distinct *popping* kind of sound, and it made both her and Tim look right directly at the crab. Before anyone could mention what had happened, the crab let go of the fish with one claw, Tim with the shock of it, let go as well, and the three of them came tumbling down through the air—one claw still holding tightly to the fish without them!

Patience felt a funny tickle in her belly as she fell, almost as though a giggle were caught in there, but before she could let it out, she was landing, rather softly in a large needlestack. She tried not to touch them, remembering her pokes and pricks at Pinny's house, though they were not nearly as sharp as those were. Quite actually, they were very slippery and she slid right off of them! Tim and the crab slid right off as well, all of them ending up on their backs and staring up at the sky, which was steely gray and looked heavy enough to rain. It was rather comfortable for them in this repose, but it was the snapping of one lone claw around a straw of hay that brought them up to sit.

"Limey beets, yeh've gone cull!" Tim exclaimed, pointing at the crab's one remaining claw. The constable snapped it with gratefulness that it was still there. "Bet yeh never thought *that* would happen."

"Course I did!" the crab argued with a bit of embarrassment. "I've done it lots of times!"

"Yeh're just saying that. It's all right. We still like yeh, don't we darling?" he said to Patience. But the little girl was not listening to their more-friendly back-and-forth. She was looking into the wide-open path at the mouth of the forest. And at the end of that path was The Wall.

They had only to hurry after her, for she was already running toward the towering canine, hoping he still remembered her.

"Excuse me!" she said to him. The wolf did not tilt his head down to look at her, but did manage to make a loud snort as though to breathe her in. He smiled widely and one gray eye afforded her a looking over.

"Oh! You're back. Got your ticket then?"

"Yes! I do!" Patience got the ticket from Tim who had just caught up and was a little out of breath from the unanticipated sprint.

"Here it is!" She waved the ticket as close to the Wall's face as she could manage, which was somewhere near his bellybutton.

"Oh, I am so glad!" And the wolf stepped down from the log he'd been standing on for so long and sat on it, taking the ticket from her. "Let's see here—" He looked it over carefully, front and back and long side and short side and then rolled it up into a tube before he looked through it.

"Oh yes! This is definitely the ticket! See?"

He handed it to Patience so she could have a look through it as well. Very clearly she could see her little missing shoe!

"But that is mine!" she said excitedly.

"You're right—it *is* yours! And you may go and get it now."

"Right now?" she asked, her mirth shadowing just a bit. She looked at the wolf and noticed that he was looking less wolf-like and a little more German shepherd-like, his ears and nose darker than she remembered and his face a little sweeter and narrower than before.

"Right now. But you'll have to take a little ride in this—" And he patted the log that he sat on, only now it was no longer a log. It was a very long and slender thing, still of wood, but it had some very taut strings running down its length and it had tuning pegs on one end and it looked very much like a citole. He saw how she was looking at it, her little eyes full of skepticism. "I'll even give you a push," he offered.

"Well," she said with some hesitation. "All right. Just let me get my friends—"

But that would just not be.

"I am sorry my little one," the Wall—now not a wall—was saying. "But your ticket only allows one person to travel in this. You see—" and he showed the writing along the edge of the ticket to her. "That is the fine print. You will have to go by yourself."

Patience's brows furrowed deeply and she felt a very hard ache in her chest. She looked at Tim and the crab, both of whom were standing just a bit away, watching, wondering what she was going to do next.

"Is that some sort of joke?" It didn't seem very fine to Patience! "Can't I hide them? Can't I take them if we pretend that I'm not?" she pleaded.

The wolf—now not a wolf—looked at her two little friends, tiny as they were really, and finally gave a little nod.

"You can try to hold onto them, my dear. But you must promise not to be disappointed when you no longer can."

"I will try," Patience said most obediently.

"Very well then."

He stood and just as Patience scooped up Tim and the crab, the German shepherd—now not a German shepherd—was scooping her up in his very strong arms and then placing her inside of the citole.

214

"Your eyes are very blue—" Patience said, noticing that the once German Shepherd-wolf-Wall was actually a black-haired, ice blue-eyed young man. He seemed not in the least startled by the fact that his eyes were not black or white or gray anymore, and the rest of their surroundings were also very quickly filling in with vibrant color.

"I guess things really aren't always black and white," Tim was stating with all obviousness.

"Not today they aren't," agreed the constable.

The man smiled at them all, his teeth still wolf-sharp behind his gentle and careful grin.

"Ready then?" he asked, and at Patience's nod, he gave the citole one very hard and firm push.

18. Sweet Treats for Sweet Dreams

Patience could scarcely catch her breath as they moved along through the trees faster than she could ever remember going at any other time of her little life. She held so tightly to little Tim and the little crab, she half feared that she would crush them in her arms and right into her chest! But as she tried, the world of the forest and the blur of growing color became smeared and damp and she felt that she was going faster and faster, until she could no longer feel her tiny companions against her. She could not feel anything except the salt in her eyes and the knot in her throat—and the odd tickling pressure against her bare foot.

And then, in a sudden breath and with a blinding exposure to the light that had not been there before, a gentle hand around her little bare ankle pulled her quite out into the open.

Patience blinked away tears, nearly forgetting the pain that had briefly come with them and sat up, warm wet curls plastered to one side of her face. She looked into the face of her sweetly smiling mother, one little white shoe in her maternal hand.

"Well, it looks like you've been off on quite an adventure, my preciousness," her mother observed gently. "You must be a bit hungry."

She presented Patience then with one of her favorite zwieback biscuits from her other hand and cuddled her up into her arms to let her awaken slowly.

They sat in silence, listening to the birds tweeting outside, their own beloved felines—one black and one white—pacing out from under the bed and purring next to them. And just from the shine in her daughter's eyes, for it had been said that such a gleam had appeared in her own from time to time, Alice knew very well *exactly* where her baby had just been.

Never... The End